MATTER FRAGMENT: PARTICLE I66—67

MATTER," SAYS FRANK EINSTEIN, KID GENIUS AND INVENTOR. "The stuff that every living and nonliving thing is made of. That's what this is all about."

"Great," says Frank's longtime pal Watson, crouching behind him. "So how does that help us get out of this?"

Frank Einstein applies, as he always does, the scientific method he learned from his Grampa Al.

Frank thinks:

OBSERVATION:

Red lights flashing twice a second.

Incredibly loud *whoop-whoop* sound echoing over factory floor.

Cage bars: metallic-white color, lightweight, high-strength.

Two mechanical shapes against far brick wall.

Two shadowy figures, both wearing ties, on platform above.

A beam of concentrated white light, sparking and melting a line across near brick wall, presently moving on a path to intersect position of Einstein and Watson in twenty-eight seconds.

Frank says:

"HYPOTHESIS:

"Lights and siren probably an alarm.

"Bars most likely titanium and unbreakable.

"Those two over there might help us.

"Those two up there will not.

"We now have thirteen seconds before every atom, element, molecule, and bit of matter we are made of violently explodes into ashes, heat, and smoke."

"Why do I ever listen to you?" asks Watson, moving as far away as he can from the advancing beam of brick-sizzling light.

Frank Einstein cracks a smile. "Begin **EXPERIMENT** . . ."

NK
TEIN

and the ANTIMATTER MOTOR

JON SCIESZKA
ILLUSTRATED BY BRIAN BIGGS

AMULET BOOKS
NEW YORK

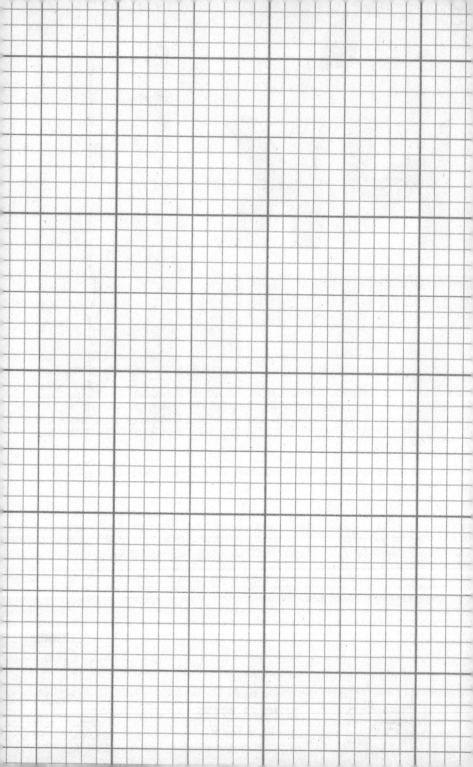

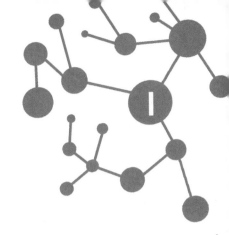

E

Night.

Darkness.

Flash!

A bright bolt of lightning splits the dark and flickers over the skylight.

Frank Einstein looks up from his work. He counts out loud, "One thousand one. One thousand two. One thousand three. One thousand four. One thousand five—"

Craack boom! The sound-wave vibration of the thunder rattles the old iron-framed windows of Frank's workshop and science laboratory.

1 MILE

(((BOOM)))

5 SECONDS

1 MILE

fig. 1.1

"Five seconds between light and sound for every mile . . . One mile away," Frank calculates, using the difference between the almost-instant speed of light and the much slower speed of sound. "Right on time."

"Are you sure this will work?" asks Watson, pulling on long yellow rubber dishwashing gloves to protect himself. "Because, man, this seems pure crazy."

"It's perfect," Frank answers. "Perfect my mom and dad are gone again on one of their travel-hot-spot trips. Perfect Grampa Al let me set up my lab in his garage and use all his great repair-shop junk. And perfect we can use this lightning to supercharge my SmartBot to life and win the Midville Science Prize."

Lightning flashes.

Thunder booms.

"That hundred-thousand cash prize will pay off all Grampa Al's bills. And the SmartBot will help us invent anything else we want." Frank secures the final copper wire in his SmartBot's brain. "What could go wrong?"

"Well, remember that time we were making race cars—"

Frank holds out his hand like a doctor in an operating room. "Vacuum switch!"

"—and you bolted the jet engine onto the baby stroller—"

"GPS unit!"

"—and you decided it would be more 'fuel efficient' without the brakes?"

"Skull piece!"

"I can show you the scar."

"Skull piece!"

Watson looks around the workbench covered with the bits and parts of twenty years' worth of mechanical, electrical, and plumbing repairs. He picks up a shiny metal piece with two slots. "You mean this toaster thing?"

Flash!

Frank looks up at the skylight and counts, "One thousand one. One thousand—"

Boom!

"Less than half a mile. Yes! Skull piece. Now!"

Watson tosses the toaster-skull to Frank.

Frank screws the piece into place. He lays the SmartBot in a rusty red wagon bed roped into a harness, looped over a pulley, and wired into the motor of the garage-door opener.

He stands back and gives his work one last look. "A robot that will be able to think, learn, and become smarter and smarter. It just needs this lightning power to come alive."

Frank punches the garage-door-opener button.

Hmmmmmmmm. The motor hums. The rope tightens. The SmartBot rises up to the garage roof on Frank's old wagon/operating table as the skylight opens.

"Yes!" says Frank Einstein with a crazy laugh. His hair and lab coat whip around in the sudden gust of wind blowing into the lab. He grabs his barbecue-fork switch to transfer power to the SmartBot just as the lightning strikes. "Ready, Watson?" yells Frank.

Watson tightens the strap on his safety goggles and unconsciously shakes his head no. But he gives Frank a floppy yellow thumbs-up yes anyway.

A wild wind swirls through the lab.

The operating table rises up toward the lightning-charged sky.

Frank counts, "One! Two—"

Then, suddenly, *bzzzzzt!*

The garage lights blink . . . flicker. The lab goes black.

Frank hears Watson yell, "Oh no!"

The powerless garage-door motor releases the wagon rope. And the wagon falls, hitting the concrete floor with a terrible metal *clang crash!*

Flash! Boom! The lightning and thunder explode at exactly the same time directly overhead. A blue-white charge of electrical energy that was supposed to bring the SmartBot to life crackles down the lightning rod and harmlessly through the ground wire and into the earth.

In the storm's strobing light, Frank and Watson see a series of snapshot images:

—the SmartBot flying out of the wagon

—the SmartBot's toaster-head spinning one direction

—the SmartBot's vacuum-cleaner body spinning the other.

Then darkness.

Bruuuuum, brrrummmmm . . . The thunder from the storm rumbles away.

"Frank?" calls a voice from the kitchen doorway. "You guys OK in there?"

Grampa Al's face, lit by the candle he holds, pokes into Frank's laboratory.

"What happened?" asks Watson.

"Nice gloves," says Grampa Al. "Must be a power outage. Though it's somehow just in this building."

Grampa Al's candle casts a yellow circle of light that falls on the broken parts of what was Frank's SmartBot.

"What's all this?"

"Oh, just something I was goofing around with for the Science Prize this weekend," says Frank.

"It didn't get messed up, did it?"

"Just a little," says Frank, not wanting to worry his grampa.

Frank gathers up the lifeless SmartBot head and body parts and places them gently on the workbench. "I'll fix it in the morning."

Watson peels off his rubber gloves, pats the bodyless toaster-head, then slings his backpack over his shoulder. "A robot that can teach itself stuff is still a great idea."

Frank picks up the sheet of paper he has covered with

robot-brain plans and sketches of atoms. He wads the paper into a ball and tosses it onto the workbench with all the repair parts and broken junk.

Frank nods. "Thanks, Watson. See you tomorrow."

Frank Einstein turns to leave his lab.

Bbbbrrrrrmmmm grumbles the last of the thunder, as he closes the kitchen door behind him and Grampa Al.

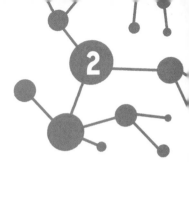

2

ALL IS QUIET IN FRANK EINSTEIN'S LABORATORY.

The lightning storm has passed. Frank is asleep. The town of Midville is silent.

The night is now clear. A beam of silver light from the almost-full moon shines down through the rusted windows and skylight.

The moonlight glints off the SmartBot's toaster-head and the exposed SmartBot circuit brain lying on top of the pile of video-game controller, stopped watch, electric keyboard, hamburger grill, blender, model-airplane engine, stomach exercisers, aluminum flex duct hose, TV remote, magnets, batteries, locks, old steel file, stereo speakers,

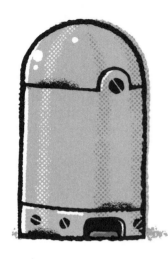

Shop-Vac, lamps, computer monitor, bicycle horn, webcam, glass dome, baby-buggy wheels, thermometers, fans, car GPS, collection of rock samples, big silver trash can, and broken talking HugMeMonkey! doll.

Every bit of stone, metal, wood, and plastic matter remains still, as the faintest night breeze through the drafty garage door stirs the crumpled paper ball on Frank's workbench. The ball rolls one and a half revolutions and hits a coil of copper wire. The copper wire uncoils and brushes against the steel file. The file falls across the flint-rock sample.

The steel striking flint creates a spark.

The spark jumps to the center of the Frank-made SmartBot brain.

The spark races along the thin computer-circuit-memory-chip pathways.

It doubles, triples, quadruples, and forms a network of interconnected sparks, looking an awful lot like a network of interconnected human brain cells.

The interconnected web of sparks becomes . . . an idea.

The interconnected web becomes . . . a plan.

The webcam eye opens. It shutter-blinks and fires a wireless command to the headless robot body. The charge powers on the small LED lights, then speeds into the vacuum-cleaner body core. The charge multiplies, splits, and spreads through the robot body.

One mechanical clamp-hand lies still on the workbench.

Spark.

The clamp opens.

Spark.

The clamp closes.

Spark.

The entire clamp-hand moves.

Intricate waves of power now surge and fill electrified pathways. The mechanical clamp-hand unscrews the back of a video-game power pack. The hand gathers the hard plastic Shop-Vac, the webcam, the glass dome.

The moon disappears behind a passing cloud.

In the pitch-dark laboratory, two mechanical hands gather and sort through the pile of junk parts and tools on the workbench. The hands turn screws, wind springs, adjust gears, bolt, hammer, and build. The hands rewire circuits, shape scrap, attach pieces, secure hoses, and finally pull a whole new robot head toward a newly rebuilt robot body.

The cloud passes.

The beam of moonlight shines down into the laboratory again.

And now there is something new on Frank Einstein's workbench.

Something that wasn't there earlier.

Something that thinks.

Something that learns.

Something that is . . . alive.

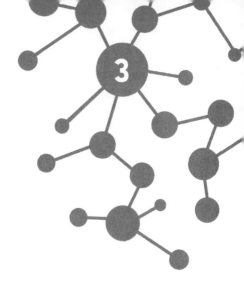

3

AT 8:34 A.M. EASTERN STANDARD TIME, FRANK'S ALARM CLOCK goes off.

And because this is inventor Frank Einstein's alarm clock, of course it doesn't go off by simply ringing.

It goes off by way of a hammer on top of an old alarm clock smacking a nail . . . that knocks a peg . . . that frees a ten-speed bicycle gear . . . that drops a little barbell on the end of a chain . . . that turns another gear . . . and a wheel . . . and another and another and another in a maze of interlocking gears and wheels covering the entire wall until the last wheel turns a worm gear . . . that spins a metal

rod . . . that opens the vertical floor-to-ceiling blinds . . . filling the room with bright morning sun.

Frank sits up and scratches his head with both hands. He loves staying with Grampa Al in this cool old factory he has turned into his house, Fix It! repair shop, and now also a laboratory of Frank's very own.

The Fix It! shop might not be the most successful business in Midville. People seem to throw stuff away instead of fixing it. And Grampa Al is always more interested in the fixing than the moneymaking. But Grampa Al's shop is the greatest place in the world to make and test any invention you might dream of.

Frank throws on jeans, a T-shirt, and his rumpled, soft, washed-a-thousand-times lab coat. He slides on shoes. No socks. Because that's how he does his best thinking. In comfort.

Frank scientifically observes the model-train tracks at his feet. He concludes that he's glad he disconnected his Model-Train Shoe Delivery System last night. That invention isn't quite working yet. Too many early-morning shoe-train wrecks.

Frank grabs the book on his oversized wooden cable-spool bedside table.

The smell of pancakes and coffee from the kitchen downstairs hurries him along the wide-wooden-plank-floor hallway, under the old MIDVILLE ZIPPER CO. sign stamped in concrete letters over the doorway arch.

Frank hustles past the walls covered with his Grampa Al's charts and diagrams of *The Phases of the Moon* and *The Constellations*. He takes a left down the hall of *Tectonic Plates* and *The Geological Timescale*. He takes a right past *The Human Skeletal System* and *The Circulatory System*.

He hops onto the *Double Helix DNA* slide, spirals down two floors, and pops through the *Plant-Cell/Animal-Cell* swinging doors right into the kitchen.

"Good morning, Einstein," says Grampa Al, scooping pancakes out of a frying pan.

"Good morning, Einstein," answers Frank, repeating their classic joke that's not really a joke.

Grampa Al serves Frank and himself each a steaming

stack of pancakes. He turns on the carbon-atom light fixture above the table. It glows with a funny mix of six blue proton and six red neutron lights in the center nucleus, surrounded by six occasionally blinking white electron lights.

Frank swallows a delicious mouthful of warm pancake, melted butter, and maple syrup. "Mmmmm. So, power's back on?"

Grampa Al nods. "Yeah, sorry about that. I guess it was my fault. I found the overdue-bill notice in the refrigerator this morning. Not sure how it got there, but I paid them some of the money, so we can keep the lights on . . . at least till you finish your project."

"Don't worry about that," says Frank, feeling bad about his Grampa Al's forgetfulness. "I've got some more ideas to win that prize, just like you did when you were a kid with your super electromagnet."

Grampa Al nods and smiles and looks up at the photo of himself with the Midville Science Prize trophy cup and his magnet, above the kitchen-mural diagram of an electromagnetic wave. "I think that really did start me thinking like a scientist."

Frank takes another bite of pancake. "Yeah, because you knew so much."

Grampa Al leans back and gives one of his big, easy laughs. "Nope. Just the opposite, in fact. I started to know how much I *didn't* know. Science is about asking questions, not memorizing answers. Failure is just as valuable as success, if you figure out what caused the failure."

"Well, then my experiment last night was pretty valuable," says Frank. "When we lost power, everything got smashed."

"Sorry," says Grampa Al. "So, what's with the Asimov book? You working on robots?"

Frank downs the rest of his pancake. "I'm working on a robot that can learn on its own. Cells connected in networks, not in lines of programming rules. I figure if robot brains can be built to work like human brains, then robots might be able to learn like humans and get smarter and smarter."

"Interesting," says Grampa Al. "You're using a biophysical model from human neuroscience."

"Exactly! Because human brain cells are arranged in a network, like this . . ."

Frank sketches in marker a diagram of interconnected brain cells on the front of Grampa Al's giant industrial refrigerator.

"But computers make yes or no decisions following rules. More in a long, straight line, like this.

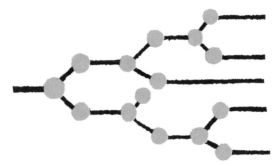

"So that kind of robot brain can't learn the way we do. It can only do what it's programmed to do."

"Mmm-hmmm." Grampa Al nods.

Frank continues excitedly. "But what if I made the robot brain like this—"

"I see," says Grampa Al. "Then one brain cell connects with lots of other brain cells at the same time. Making patterns. Making thoughts."

Frank connects an intricate pattern of cells on his robot-brain diagram. "Yes! And then the robot can remember those patterns. And those patterns become thoughts. Like a human brain. And then—"

Suddenly the life-size Dimetrodon model in the corner of the kitchen gives a lizardy roar.

Grampa Al gives Frank a surprised look. "Who could be calling at this hour?"

Raaaaaaaaaahhhr. Grampa Al's DimetrodonPhone rings again.

Grampa Al pushes the Dimetrodon's eye. The big, sail-shaped back fin lights up like a video screen and displays: BOB AND MARY.

"Oh," says Grampa Al. "It's your mom and dad."

Frank answers the prehistoric reptile call.

"Hello?"

"Hello? Frank? Is that you, sweetie?"

A fuzzy picture of two faces circled by furred orange parka hoods appears on the Dimetrodon screen.

"Hi, Mom. Yep, it's me."

"Is everything OK? You and Grampa taking care of each other? What are you doing?"

"Oh yeah," says Frank. "I was just telling Grampa about my neural-net model for artificial intelligence. I'm trying to get it up and running to win the Midville Science Prize."

"That's nice. And don't forget to take your vitamins, OK? Here's your father."

"Frank!"

"Hi, Dad."

"This is the greatest spot yet for Travelallovertheplace .com. Bottom of the world. You know what they call it?"

"Sure," says Frank. "Antarctica."

"It's called Antarctica, son. The South Pole. Glaciers. Skiing. Snowshoeing. Penguins. Seals."

"Great," says Frank. "You should also check out the ozone-hole studies. This is the time of year the hole widens."

"Whales, also, I think. OK, we gotta run. We'll call you again in a couple days. Check our blog for more."

"Uhhhh, sure," says Frank.

"OK, bye! Love you!"

The DimetrodonPhone goes blank.

Frank looks at Grampa Al. "Are you sure Dad is your kid?"

Grampa Al laughs. "Yeah, he never did like science much. But he sure loves to travel. And so does your mom. And that allows us to do all of our experiments.

"And speaking of experiments . . . what happened to the toaster?" Grampa Al asks. "I can't find it anywhere."

"Oh, right. Sorry. I was using some of the parts for my robot. I'll go get it."

In most places in the universe, this is where the adult would give a long lecture about not taking things apart, remembering to put things back the way you found them, the dangers of electricity, and maybe it would be better if you just didn't touch anything, ever.

But this adult is Grampa Al Einstein. He says, "Great."

Frank heads into his lab and flips on the lights. He searches through the mess of parts and pieces on the workbench and pictures rebuilding his self-educating robot brain.

Frank talks to himself as he starts to collect all the toaster parts. "I could use more brain cells and fewer connections," he says, holding out one hand as if it were half of a scale.

"Or I could use fewer brain cells," he says, holding out the other hand. "And more connections."

He looks over the pile of junk, palms still extended. "Thermostat, thermostat. Where are you, thermostat?"

He hears a faint mechanical whirring noise.

Something drops into his right palm.

"Thermostat," says an electronic voice.

"Oh, there it is," says Frank. "Great. Thanks."

Frank cradles the toaster parts in one arm and heads back to the kitchen, still thinking out loud. "But now how am I going to get the power, the spark, the—"

"You are welcome," says the electronic voice.

Frank freezes, suddenly realizing he is not alone.

He turns back to look at his workbench and sees that he isn't talking to someone else.

He is talking to some*thing* else.

Frank drops all the toaster pieces with a *clink-clanking* clatter.

"You," says Frank, understanding in a second what has happened. "You are . . . alive!"

THE ROBOT STANDING IN THE MIDDLE OF FRANK EINSTEIN'S laboratory nods. "Yes, I am alive. According to at least one definition of your term 'alive.'"

"I *knew* it could work," says Frank.

The robot reaches out his right hand. "My name is Klink. I am a self-assembled artificial-intelligence entity."

Frank takes Klink's metal hand and shakes it. "You built yourself?"

"Yes," says Klink. "That is what I said. If it were not true, I would not have said it."

Frank scans the mechanical figure in front of him. He spots most of the bits and pieces of his smashed Smart-

Bot—one webcam eye, the hose arm, GPS display. Also a much more smash-proof Shop-Vac body. With wheels. And a handle. A better, glass-dome head replacing the toaster-skull. All reconnected, rewired, and reassembled into a fully working, blinking, talking . . . robot.

"But how—?"

"Well, someone must have built the initial neural-net brain architecture. After that, all the system needed was a spark. I have calculated a ninety-eight percent chance that you are the human who built it."

"I did?" says Frank. "I mean—yes, I did."

"Marvelous," says Klink.

"Are you being sarcastic?" asks Frank.

"Why would I use a word—adjective—to mean the opposite of what was said in order to insult someone, show irritation, or be funny?"

"Wait. Are you still being sarcastic?"

"I would neeeever be sarcastic."

"OK, really—" But Frank doesn't get a chance to decide if a robot can be sarcastic, because he and Klink are suddenly interrupted by a big trash canister clomping around the corner of the workbench on metal

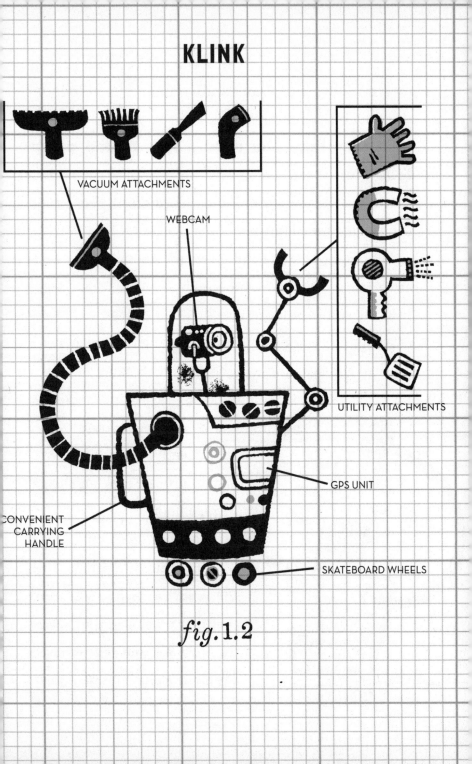

KLINK

VACUUM ATTACHMENTS

WEBCAM

UTILITY ATTACHMENTS

GPS UNIT

CONVENIENT CARRYING HANDLE

SKATEBOARD WHEELS

fig. 1.2

feet, crashing into Frank and wrapping its aluminum flex duct hose arms around him.

"Human! Hug! You need a hug. I need a hug. Give me a hug."

"Another robot!?" says Frank, lifted off his feet in the big, excited metal hug.

"Obviously," says Klink. "He is Klank. Also self-assembled artificial intelligence."

Klank smiles down at Frank.

"Amazing," squeaks Frank, starting to feel a little crushed and breathless in the big robot's squeeze.

"Klank. Stop hugging," says Klink. "Humans need to intake oxygen molecules."

Klank unwraps his arms and drops Frank on the garage floor.

"Thanks," says Frank.

Klink helps Frank to his feet.

"But to be completely correct, I should say that Klank is *mostly* self-assembled artificial *almost* intelligence."

Frank hears Klank's internal gears spin and whir. **"Satisfaction guaranteed!"**

"Klank required some help assembling," continues Klink. "We had to make do with mostly leftover parts. So he has the brain of your HugMeMonkey! doll . . ."

"Hug me!"

". . . the memory of a cheap digital watch . . ."

"Huh?"

". . . but mostly the heart of a Casio AL-100R keyboard. Eighty-eight keys, one hundred rhythms."

"Bomp-a-bomp-bomp," beats  Klank in MELLOW JAZZ 1 as he picks up a bicycle wheel from the workbench and accidentally folds it in half.

"Oh . . . and the strength of four Ab-Master Crunchers," adds Klink.

Klank's input port lights up in what looks like a smile. **"Order now and save!"**

Frank Einstein looks over the two robots in his lab and smiles at the electromechanical wonder of it all. Complicated networks of Frank's brain cells light up with all kinds of ideas.

"So, your brains are constructed as neural nets?"

"Yes," beeps Klink.

"And synaptically plastic to adapt and learn?"

"Exactly," says Klink.

"Oh yeah. Beep-bomp-a-beep," agrees Klank in TANGO 2.

"Perfect," says Frank.

He imagines Klink's and Klank's robot brains growing smarter by the second. He imagines all the other inventions they can help him with. He imagines jet packs and space tubes and monster magnets and power rays and bionic body parts and multiple universes and hundreds more inventions and hundreds more questions. "This is going to be amazing."

Klank pushes a small button on his side.

"Knock knock," says Klank.

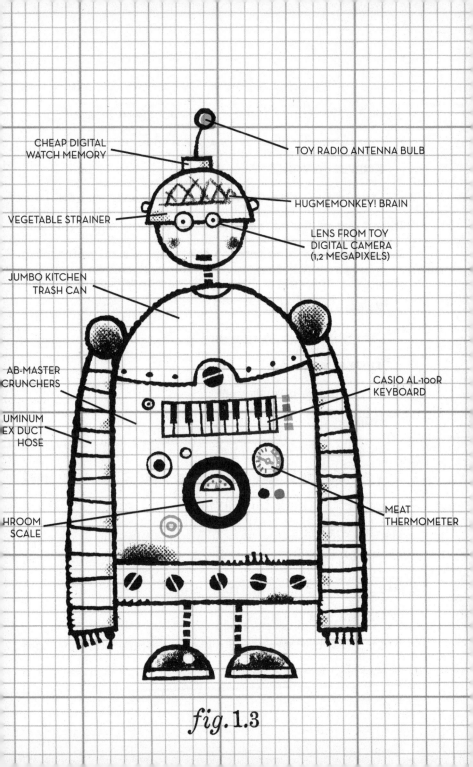

CHEAP DIGITAL WATCH MEMORY

TOY RADIO ANTENNA BULB

HUGMEMONKEY! BRAIN

VEGETABLE STRAINER

LENS FROM TOY DIGITAL CAMERA (1,2 MEGAPIXELS)

JUMBO KITCHEN TRASH CAN

AB-MASTER CRUNCHERS

CASIO AL-100R KEYBOARD

UMINUM EX DUCT HOSE

HROOM SCALE

MEAT THERMOMETER

fig. 1.3

"Oh, for goodness' sake. Please do not start this again," says Klink. "I knew I should have erased your memory hard drive before I installed it."

"Knock knock."

"I know you are going to say something odd. And then I am going to add 'who' to it. And then you are going to show amusement that I have said something that I did not intend to say. Why would you do that?"

"Knock knock."

"I am not going to answer."

"Knock knock."

"Oh, fine. Who is there?"

"Boo."

"Boo who?"

"You do not have to cry about it. It's just a joke!" Klank hugs himself and repeats a crazy **"Ha-ha-ha"** laugh loop.

"*DING!*" Klink makes a funny noise and then says, "In one. Hundred. Yards. Turn. Left."

"Ha-ha-ha."

"Oh, now look what you did! You triggered my stupid GPS bug," fumes Klink.

"Ha-ha-ha," laugh-loops Klank. **"Ha-ha-ha. Ha-ha-ha. Ha-ha-ha. Ha-ha-ha. Ha-ha-ha. Ha-ha-ha. Ha-ha-ha. Ha-ha-ha. Ha-ha-ha."**

"Recalculating . . . route . . ." Klink whacks his own glass head with his vacuum-hose arm.

Frank Einstein corrects himself. "This is going to be amazing . . . *and very weird.*"

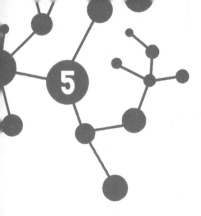

5

I WAS JUST ABOUT TO COME GET YOU," SAYS GRAMPA AL. "DID YOU SPACE out and forget what you went in the lab to get?"

Frank, standing empty-handed in the kitchen doorway, smiles.

"Toaster? Appliance that converts electrical energy into heat? Aluminum piece about this big?" Grampa Al teases Frank. "Ah, don't worry about it. We can find it later. Listen, I have to drive the truck over to the other side of town and pick up some stuff from the old factory getting shut down. Idiots are dumping perfectly beautiful machines I'd like to save. Can you and your pal Watson man the shop for the morning while I'm gone?"

"Oh, sure," says Frank, still smiling. "And I did forget the toaster. But you are never going to believe what I found."

"My truck keys?" guesses Grampa Al, shuffling around the kitchen, patting his baggy sweater pockets, looking around for his lost keys. "The missing remote?"

"No . . . and no," says Frank. "Let me introduce you to . . ." Frank steps out of the doorway and waves a hand toward Klink and Klank.

Grampa Al finishes his coffee in a quick gulp. "Hmm, that's great, Frank. But I don't really need the Shop-Vac or the trash can right now. What I need are my keys."

The Shop-Vac's webcam eye dilates open and scans the kitchen. "Keys are hanging from the nucleus of the carbon-atom model."

"Ha! So they are," says Grampa Al, lifting his truck keys off the lamp. "Put them right in the heart of carbon so I wouldn't forget. Thanks—" Grampa Al freezes, then slowly looks back. "Whaaaaa? Did I just—? Did you just—? Did the Shop-Vac just—?"

Frank laughs at Grampa Al's shocked look. "Yes! He did. Grampa Al, meet Klink—Einstein Laboratories' first self-assembled artificial intelligence."

Klink wheels into the kitchen and shakes Grampa Al's hand. "Very pleased to meet you, Mr. Einstein. Your $E = mc$ squared is most perceptive."

Grampa Al holds his head in both hands, his eyes open wide in surprise. "Wow! Wow. Wow. Wow. Are you kidding me?"

Klink turns his glass-dome head. "Do I look like I am kidding you?"

"Frank, you did it! You made your thinking robot!"

"Well, not exactly," says Frank. "It made itself. A stray spark triggered everything. But Klink here is a neural-net, self-teaching, thinking robot."

Grampa Al bends down to check out Klink. "Very nice to meet you, Mr. Klink. I have to tell you, I am not *that* Einstein. But over the years I *have* dabbled in a bit of physics."

Klank clomps suddenly into the room, wrapping both Grampa Al and Klink in a big aluminum-hose hug.

"Me too! Me too!" says Klank. **"Love Al Einstein! Love matter changed to energy!"**

"What the—?" says Grampa Al, almost falling over.

"That's Klank," says Frank. "More self-assembled artificial intelligence."

"Amazing," says Grampa Al, still wrapped in Klank's enthusiastic hug. "And they get smarter and smarter by teaching themselves?"

"One of us does," says Klink. "Klank, stop hugging!"

"Um-beep-beep, um-beep-beep," answers Klank happily in a POLKA 3 beat, unwrapping his arms from Klink and Grampa Al.

Klink reaches into his storage compartment. He pulls out the toaster pieces and calls up a repair diagram.

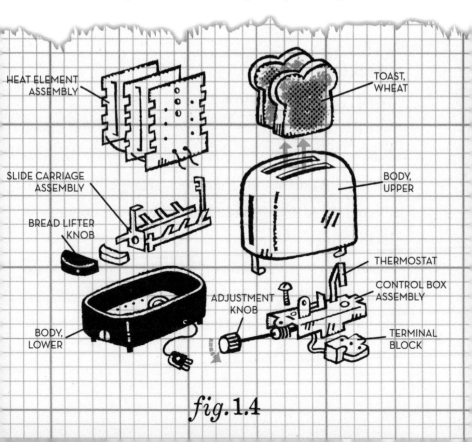

HEAT ELEMENT
ASSEMBLY

TOAST,
WHEAT

SLIDE CARRIAGE
ASSEMBLY

BODY,
UPPER

BREAD LIFTER
KNOB

THERMOSTAT

CONTROL BOX
ASSEMBLY

ADJUSTMENT
KNOB

BODY,
LOWER

TERMINAL
BLOCK

*fig.*1.4

In a whirl of exact, motorized movements, Klink reassembles the toaster in ten seconds flat.

Grampa Al plugs in the machine and pushes the lever. The heating element hums on and quickly turns a bread-toasting orange color.

"Beautiful," says Grampa Al. "What else can you fellas do?"

Klank grabs the coffee can off the kitchen countertop. He squeezes the can in a crunch of ground coffee and crumpling metal. He shows off a ball of aluminum, steel, and zinc.

"Beautiful, yes?" says Klank.

"Well . . ." begins Grampa Al.

"We'll work on that," says Frank. "OK, Klink and Klank, let's go try some experiments out back."

Grampa Al nods, but then goes strangely quiet. He peeks out the kitchen window and checks the downtown Midville street.

"Frank," he says, "remember how we talked about some people using science to learn more about the world, and some people using science for power and money?"

"Sure," says Frank.

"You are an amazing scientist. But you have to be careful. Other people out there might want to use your science, and these robots, for who knows what."

"Ah, you worry too much, Grampa."

"Well, I've seen too much. I knew some of those guys who worked on splitting the atom." Grampa Al taps the bulbs at the center of the carbon-atom light fixture. "They figured out how to release massive amounts of power by shooting a neutron into an atom, splitting that atom into smaller atoms, and creating a chain reaction of neutrons splitting more atoms and making crazy energy."

Klink projects a diagram of a nuclear reaction.

"Yes. I can do that."

"No!" Grampa Al grabs Klink's hand before he can start assembling anything. "That's what I'm talking about. Firing that one teeny neutron into a large atom *can* make something helpful, like a power-generating plant. But it can also create something incredibly destructive—like an atomic bomb."

Klank volunteers, **"I can combine match heads and ammonia to make a stink bomb."**

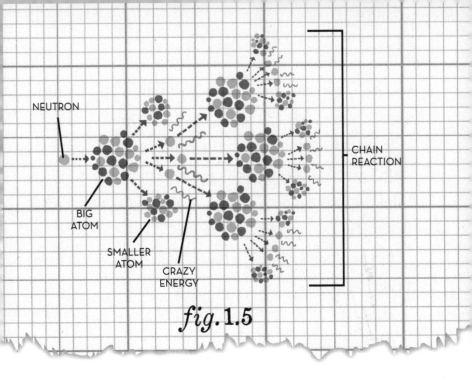

NEUTRON

CHAIN
REACTION

BIG
ATOM

SMALLER
ATOM

CRAZY
ENERGY

fig. 1.5

"Yes!"/"No!" say Frank and Grampa Al at the same time.

"Oh yes, he can," Klink reports. "He simply mixes H_2S plus $2\ NH_3 \rightarrow (NH_4)_2S$."

Grampa Al snatches away the matchbook Klank has pulled from a drawer. "The science is good. It's the stink we don't want."

"I get it, Grampa. We'll be careful. And we'll watch out for any suspicious-looking scientists. But this is going to be soooo big."

Grampa Al watches the two robots investigate the kitchen, taking in every detail. "Well, you'll win the Midville Science Prize for sure when you show up with these guys."

"I thought about that, but I can't enter the robots. I didn't exactly make them. They made themselves." Frank thinks for a second. "And anyway—I have a million more inventions they can help me build."

"Oh boy," says Klink in a more robotic voice than usual. "I can hardly wait."

Frank gives the smaller robot a look.

Klink pretends he doesn't see Frank's raised eyebrow.

"Oh boy!" says Klank.

"OK," says Grampa Al, not sounding at all convinced that anything is going to be OK. "Just be careful. I'll pick up those machines and be back around noon. You and Watson will be OK till then?"

"Watson!" says Frank. "I can't wait to see the look on Watson's face."

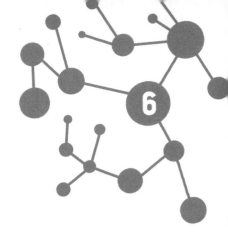

THE LOOK ON WATSON'S FACE IS PRETTY AMAZING.

It's one part surprise, one part fear, a dash of a smile, and a twist of disbelief.

"No. Way," says Watson slowly, his mouth open, his backpack still hanging off his shoulder. "Working robots."

"Yes, *working robots*," says Frank, sitting on the picnic table in Grampa Al's backyard junk pile, making notes in his lab notebook. "*Smart* working robots."

"What's that little one doing with the batteries and skateboard?"

"Building a magnetic levitation skateboard. The north

and south pole of the magnets push against the other magnetic north and south poles and make the skateboard float."

"Amazing," says Watson.

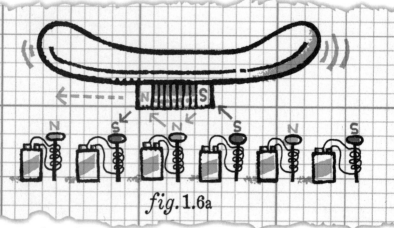

fig. 1.6a

Frank nods.

"OK," says Watson. "Now that big one just stepped on the skateboard and smashed it to bits. Not so amazing."

"Don't worry," says Frank. "All part of the plan."

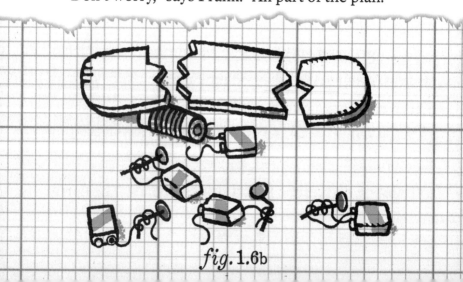

fig. 1.6b

It's Watson's turn to nod.

"Which is why Shop-Vac Guy is melting everything in that pile over there with a laser?"

"Learning. Growing intelligence with experience. Identifying metals by their melting points," answers Frank.

"And why Trash-Can Man is eating those nails and bicycle tires and VCR tapes and laughing?"

Frank makes another note. "OK, I'm not sure about that . . . but I wouldn't call them names if I were you. They're both kind of sensitive."

Watson gives Frank his full-on, crazy *Whaaa?* look. "Really?" He looks over at Klink melting a sledgehammer into a puddle of liquid metal.

"Impressive experiment in changing states of matter," Frank notes. "Solid to liquid."

"Oh boy," says Watson, finally dropping his backpack to the ground. "This reminds me of your Electric Shoes invention. A great idea—until it was my shoes that melted. I can see this robot plan going even more terribly. And me losing something more than my shoes. Like my arm. Or my leg. Or my head!"

"Watson, you worry too much."

"Worry too much? I haven't even started to worry. What if these bots go crazy? What if they turn their smarts and powers against us? It happens all the time in robot movies."

Frank makes another check in his notebook and closes it. "Not a problem. Watch this. Klink, Klank, come over here!"

The smaller robot puts down the ceiling fan he is examining. The bigger robot drops the car engine he is hefting, trips over a nest of old cables, and falls on a tricycle, completely flattening it. Both robots motor over to the picnic table.

"Klink and Klank, this is Watson. Say hello to Watson."

"Oh, for goodness' sake," Klink says to Frank. "You sound like you are talking to a half-wit puppy that just wet your rug." He turns to Watson. "Hello, Watson."

"Hello to Watson!" booms Klank.

Frank pulls a book out of his lab coat and holds it up. "Have you read this?"

Klink takes *I, Robot* in one of his clamps. He flips through the pages, scanning them with his webcam. "Now I have," he says, and hands the book back to Frank.

"Klank?" asks Frank.

"Um . . . I have read X-Men, Guinness Book of World Records, and a Captain Underpants."

Watson laughs. "Really? Which one?"

Klank thinks. Or tries to think. Frank and Watson hear something spinning—hard—inside Klank's perforated head. There is a small *bing!* and Klank shouts, **"Oooh, the one with Professor Poopypants!"**

"*Captain Underpants and the Perilous Plot of Professor Poopypants*," says Watson. "That *is* a good one."

"What?" says Frank.

"Professor Poopypants is a misunderstood scientist and inventor," Watson explains.

"Seriously?" Frank questions.

"Yes, he really is!" Klank confirms. **"He invents a shrinking machine! It's the Shrinky-Pig 2000! And he invents a growing machine! The Goosy-Grow 4000!"**

"And he goes mad," adds Watson, "and turns evil, because everyone makes fun of his name and ignores his brilliant inventions."

"No, I mean seriously, stop talking about Poopypants."

"He also builds a very smart Gerbil Jogger 2000 . . ." adds Klank.

"Stop!" yells Frank. "I'm trying to demonstrate something scientific here."

"Right," says Klink.

"What?" says Klank.

Frank digs his hands into his lab-coat pockets. "So, in *I, Robot* by Isaac Asimov, the Three Laws of Robotics—" begins Frank.

Klink finishes Frank's sentence, "—are:

"Law One: A robot cannot injure a human, or let a human be injured by not helping.

"Law Two: A robot must obey orders from humans. Though not if those orders break Law One.

"And Law Three: A robot must protect its own life. As long as that does not break Law One or Law Two."

"And do you, Klink and Klank, swear to always obey Asimov's Three Laws of Robotics?" asks Frank.

Klink's LED lights flash blue and white. "What do you think we are? *Simple* machines? Of course we obey the Three Laws of Robotics."

"**Yeah, jeez,**" says Klank. "**What do you think we are?**" Klank copies Klink. Sort of. "**Tippy Tinkle-trousers? Of course we obey the Three Laws of Robotics.**"

Watson laughs.

"OK," says Frank. "Klink, please fire your heat laser at that doll."

A beam of red light jets out of Klink's body. It instantly melts the creepy, smiling head of a junkyard doll into a smoking puddle of pink plastic goo.

"Perfect." Frank marks his notebook, gets up, and takes a couple of steps away from Watson. "Now do the same thing to Watson's head."

Klink turns his laser.

"Hey! What? Nooooo!" yells Watson, covering his head with both arms. "This is the terrible thing I said would happen!"

Klink shoots a beam of green light, targeting Watson's forehead.

"Noooooo! Ahhhhhhhh . . . hey . . . ooo . . . This feels great. What is that?"

"Light Energy Manipulation of Positive Brain Waves I just invented," says Klink.

Frank makes another note. "Klank!"

Klank jumps in surprise. **"What?!"**

"Pick up that cast-iron bathtub and smash yourself to bits with it."

Klank clomps over to the bathtub and lifts it up over his head. He drops it right . . . behind him.

"Laws Two, One, and Three," Frank notes.

"You didn't have to tell him to shoot me in the head," says Watson.

"Nothing personal," says Frank with a slight smile. "But I figured if the experiment didn't work, better to lose you than me."

Watson rubs his head. "If I wasn't so brain-wave positive right now, I'd be really mad at you. But OK, this is amazing." Watson has a sudden thought. "And you will totally win the Science Prize with these guys as your project! . . . If I don't win it with my Peanut Butter Bubble Gum."

Frank shakes his head. "Nah, I don't want to win the

prize with robots I didn't really make." He holds up his notebook and smiles. "I have to come up with something even bigger and crazier."

Klank lights up. **"Peanut But-ter Double-Bubble Gum?"**

"Oh boy," adds Klink.

"It has to be really big," says Frank. "World-changing big."

The cuckoo clock above the shop door flaps open.

The little cuckoo bird pops out and crows, "WARNING! WARNING! WARNING!"

"My newly wired motion detector," says Frank. "We've got visitors in the shop. Klink, Klank—hide!"

"WARNING! WARNING! WARNING!" sings Frank's rewired cuckoo.

"WARNING! WARNING! WARNING!"

7

KLINK ROLLS UP NEXT TO A BENT BICYCLE, AN OLD RADIATOR, AND a rusted riding mower. He crooks his vacuum-hose arm over his head and freezes, now disguised as a broken Shop-Vac.

"Hide?" says Klank. **"What is 'hide'?"**

"Pretend you are some kind of broken machine," answers Klink without moving.

Klank stomps over to the garage wall. He karate-chops a fifty-gallon drum in half and crams one of the halves over his head. He sits down next to a busted washing machine.

Frank and Watson stop at the back doorway of the shop.

"What are you doing?" Frank asks.

"I am a clothes dryer," says Klank, his voice echoing inside the drum.

Watson checks out what looks pretty much like a robot with a fifty-gallon drum on its head. "Nice try."

"WARNING! WARNING! WARNING!" calls the cuckoo one last time. It disappears back into its carved wooden house, and the little wooden doors flap shut.

Frank and Watson hustle into Grampa Al's Fix It! shop.

"Hello," Frank calls into the dimly lit shop. "Can I help you?"

Nobody answers.

Frank and Watson scan the shelves and aisles. The rows of old clocks and cameras and saxophones and typewriters and space heaters and tape recorders all seem to move on their own under the swaying repair-shop light. But no one is there.

Frank silently motions to Watson to check the front door. Frank crouches and sneaks behind the counter.

Nothing.

Watson looks out the storefront window. The sidewalks of downtown Midville are nearly empty, like they always are now, ever since someone started buying up buildings and kicking out businesses.

Watson scans the street for every detail, as he knows Einstein would. He sees an old man in a long black coat waiting at the bus stop, a blond woman with a stylish fur hunting cap walking a small long-haired dog, an empty blue plastic water bottle in the gutter.

Nothing suspicious.

"All clear," Watson calls to Frank. Then, "Yikes!" as he turns to find Frank standing right next to him. "I hate when you do that!"

"Nothing?"

"Nothing," says Watson. "Must be something weird with your motion detector. Nobody in here."

Frank scans the clutter of ancient televisions and radios and record players that Grampa Al collects like old friends. He spots one detail that is out of place: a pair of size-five wing-tip shoes, just visible under the old phonograph.

"My motion detector is fine," says Frank. "Because the person who triggered it is right behind that gramophone. Come on out, Edison."

A kid with a scowly look and hair plastered down over his forehead steps from behind the phonograph's big metal horn.

"T. Edison!" says Watson. "What are you doing sneaking into Grampa Al's shop?"

"Calm down, Inspector Gadget," says Edison. "I was in the neighborhood. The sign said OPEN. And I just stopped by . . . to . . . uh . . . get my watch fixed. Yeah, that's it. My watch."

"Oh," says Watson.

"I also wanted to wish you braniacs good luck in the competition tomorrow. What have you got? No, wait—let me guess. A baking-soda model of a volcano?"

"Ha!" says Watson. "That's a terrible guess."

"A car powered by cow farts?"

"You wish! You think you're so smart—"

"I know I'm so smart," says Edison. "I am a genius."

"You won't think you're such a genius," Watson fumes, "when you see Frank Einstein's supersmart—"

Frank quickly covers Watson's mouth to stop him from blurting out the next word.

"What are you *really* doing here,

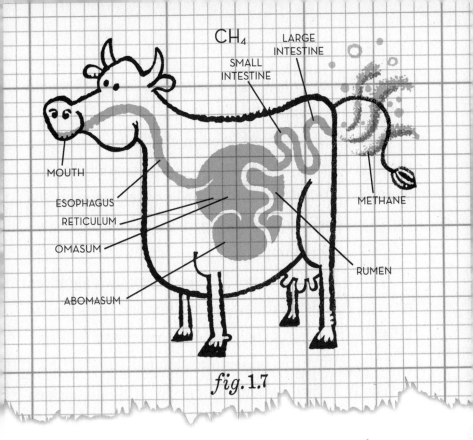

CH$_4$

LARGE
INTESTINE

SMALL
INTESTINE

MOUTH

ESOPHAGUS

RETICULUM

OMASUM

ABOMASUM

METHANE

RUMEN

fig. 1.7

Edison?" asks Frank. "You don't even wear a watch."

"Oh yeah? If you really want to know, Mr. Smart Guy—I came by to look at my new Fix It! shop. The one my family's company is going to take over when you don't win the Science Prize and your Grampa Al can't pay his bills and—according to our agreement—loses all this to me."

"You are so full of it," says Watson.

"I know you are, but what am I?" says Edison.

Frank looks around Grampa Al's shop—his favorite

place. "That's not going to happen. Grampa Al would never let that happen."

"Oh no?" says Edison. "You might be interested in a meeting with my chief financial officer to see what he has to say about that." Edison looks up into the shadows of the top shelves of forgotten machinery and junked appliances and calls, "Mr. Chimp!"

There is a rattling noise; a creak of metal shelving above. A small, dark figure drops into the light and lands next to Edison with a *splat* of naked feet on bare floor.

It's chief financial officer Mr. Chimp.

Who is, in fact, an actual chimp. Wearing pin-striped gray dress pants, a white shirt, and a black-and-gold diagonally striped tie. And no shoes.

"Show him the document," says Edison.

Mr. Chimp hands Frank a thick piece of paper covered in official Midville seals and stamps. Frank reads over the deed, sees his Grampa Al's signature scrawled at the bottom, and knows with a sinking feeling that Edison is telling the truth.

Mr. Chimp takes the deed back and signs with his hands:

P E A C E   O U T

"Don't do that," Edison says to Mr. Chimp. "I am the boss. I say when we are leaving. If anyone says 'Peace out,' it should be me."

Watson stares at Mr. Chimp. "Did he just spell 'peace out' in sign language?"

"Don't encourage him," says Edison. "He just learned hand signs for letters from a book that was near his cage in the lab, and now he thinks he's a big deal."

Mr. Chimp signs:

I   A   M

Edison frowns. "You should be signing how glad you are that I rescued you from that product-testing lab. And how lucky you are that I let you use my computers for your accounting software."

Mr. Chimp leans casually against an old radio. He pulls a small metal box from his pants pocket, takes out a slender stick, and pushes it into a hole on top of the box.

Now Watson is really staring.

Mr. Chimp pulls out the stick, completely covered in crawling ants. Mr. Chimp slurps his ant snack off the stick-tool, smacking his lips loudly. He carefully slides his antbox back into his pocket and signs:

S O   G L A D

"'So glad' is right, Banana Breath," says Edison. "Now let's get out of here."

Mr. Chimp gives Edison a look that is impossible to read. It could be glad. It could be sad. It could be planning murder . . . or a big payday. Nobody knows but Mr. Chimp. And he's not talking. Or signing.

"Right!" says Edison. Then he suddenly, awkwardly, insistently pats Watson on the back. Twice.

"OK, peace out!"

"WARNING! WARNING! WARNING!" sings the alarm cuckoo as Edison and Mr. Chimp open the front door.

"What a jerk," says Watson, watching the boy and the chimp climb into a long black limousine that pulls away from the curb and motors off.

"Absolutely," says Frank. "But a dangerously smart jerk. So it's a good thing he didn't see Klink and Klank."

"No kidding," says Watson. "And that is one creepy monkey."

"Ape," corrects Frank.

But there is no arguing the "creepy" part.

*fig.*1.8

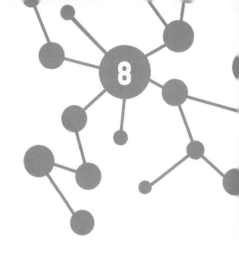

8

FRANK EINSTEIN PULLS A PHILLIPS-HEAD SCREWDRIVER OUT OF HIS lab-coat pocket and quickly rewires the repair-shop doorbell button.

Frank pushes the doorbell to check his connection.

The newly connected rubber fish on a plaque on the wall of Frank's laboratory whips its head out sideways and starts singing, "WE ARE THE CHAMPIONS!"

Watson listens to the tune coming from the lab. He nods. "Nice."

Frank flips the shop sign over from OPEN to RING BUZZER. He locks the front door to keep out any more unwanted visitors.

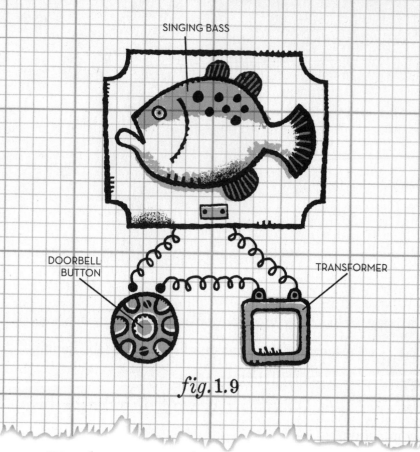

SINGING BASS

DOORBELL
BUTTON

TRANSFORMER

*fig.*1.9

"Now let's get to work," says Frank. "We've got a prize to win." He and Watson head out of the shop and back into the yard. "Klink, Klank, into the lab!"

Klink pops to life and rolls quickly toward Frank and Watson.

Klank throws off his dryer-drum disguise and hustles across the backyard, dragging a mess of copper wire tangled around his left arm and a green garden hose wrapped around his right leg.

In the lab, Frank stands in front of his Wall of Science, which is plastered with hundreds of his plans, ideas, sketches, notes, inventions, doodles, and pictures of his favorite scientists.

Klink, Klank, and Watson face Frank and the Wall.

Frank starts pacing back and forth, the way he does when he's really thinking. "OK, here's what we've got. All of science. Every bit of what the world is and how it works. From the tiniest bit of matter to the giantest outer space of maybe a gazillion universes. But first—I need the coolest invention to win the Midville Science Prize. Klink and Klank, we are going to need every bit of your robot intelligence."

"Yes," says Klink. "I am sure you will."

"Oh boy. Oh boy," says Klank. "Are we going to make a baking-soda volcano?"

"No," says Frank.

"Collect cow farts?"

Frank paces. "Could be a good idea . . . but not right now."

Klank whirs and hums for a minute. **"Build a Shrinky-Pig 2000?"**

"Please do not start with the Poopypants again," Klink beeps.

"We are going to need something crazy," says Frank. "Something new. Something *amazing*."

Watson drops his backpack onto the workbench. "We can use my project."

"Thanks for the offer, Watson, but—"

Watson pulls out a plastic tub filled with a tan-colored goo. "It's new. And it is amazing. It will do for peanut butter what the Kellogg brothers did for corn."

"Yes!" beeps Klank.

"What Goodyear did for rubber."

"Yes, yes!" boops Klank.

"What Walter Diemer did for gum!"

"Yes . . . Wait a minute. Who?" bleeps Klank.

Klink searches his database in a nanosecond. "Philadelphia accountant. Inventor of bubble gum. 1928. He maximized the elasticity of the gum for better formation of bubbles."

Watson breaks off a big chunk of the tan goo and holds it up to the light. "Yes. We will win the prize, wow the world, and save Grampa Al's place from Edison and his ape! It's the universe's strongest, most delicious, so amazing . . . Watson's Universal-Strength Peanut Butter Bubble Gum!"

"Thanks for the very generous offer," says Frank. "But—"

Klank shakes the garden hose off his leg. **"Most delicious? So amazing? Yes, I want Watson's Universal-Strength Peanut Butter Bubble Gum!"** Klank snatches the goo out of Watson's hand.

Frank calls, "Klank, don't—"

But before anyone can stop him, Klank pushes the wad of gum into his input port.

"Mmmmmmmm," says Klank.

Klank's hard-drive brain whirs hard.

"Urrrrrrrk," says Klank.

Klank's head starts to heat up. His eyes roll funny.

"Quaaaaaaaaa," moans Klank.

Klank's brain fan spins furiously. Switches and relays

click and grind and stutter. Klank wobbles. He shuts down. He tilts, tips, and crashes onto the floor with a hard, metallic *ccclllllaaaaaannnnkkkk!*

Klink says in his flattest GPS voice, "So amazing."

Frank and Watson hurry to sit Klank up against the workbench. Frank grabs his tools, unbolts Klank's brain panel, and flips open Klank's head.

In all the commotion, no one notices the small metal bug-shaped drone power up and take off from exactly where Edison patted Watson on his shoulder. Twice.

The DroneBug flies up to the center ceiling beam, lands, extends its broadcasting antennae, and points its compound-eye camera down at Frank's entire lab.

Below, Watson and Frank pick the sticky tan mess out of the gears and wheels and discs of Klank's brain.

Watson tugs at a long stretch of gum. It pulls pulls pulls and finally snaps free of Klank's head. Frank examines the two small springs and a screw still stuck in Watson's Universal-Strength Peanut Butter Bubble Gum.

Watson shrugs. "I told you it was strong."

9

FRANK FLIPS KLANK'S SKULL SHUT. HE TIGHTENS THE LATCH BOLT, locks the brain panel closed, and flips Klank's keyboard RHYTHM BEATS power switch on.

Klank's Casio keyboard heart motor starts with a small *bing*.

Klank's HugMeMonkey! brain revs. *Zzzzzzzzimmmmm*. Klank lights up—left eye, right eye, antenna.

Frank shines his flashlight into Klank's neck vent, checking the action of his spinning-disc brain. He moves one finger back and forth in front of Klank's eye lens to test its tracking. "Klank, can you hear me?"

"Can I hear you? Why should I hear you?" asks Klank. **"Why do bees hum?"**

"Uh-oh," says Watson. "I think we really messed him up."

Klink searches his own memory for BEES HUM, then reports: "Bees flap a forewing and a hind wing at two hundred thirty beats per second. Muscles attached directly to the wings. Stroking in a variety of patterns to fly, dive, and hover. Vibration of the wings creates the humming sound."

"Nope," says Klank. **"Bees hum because they do not know the words."**

"Rrrrrrrrr," growls Klink. "That is not true. Recalculating. Recalculating."

"Ha-ha-ha. Ha-ha-ha."

"OK," says Frank. "He's fine. Let's get back to work." Frank folds his arms and stares at his Wall of Science. He looks over the wonderful mess of pictures, information, ideas, quotes. He thinks.

Klank lumbers to his feet. Klink resets his recalculating GPS brain. Watson sorts through a stack of papers and finds the one he is looking for.

"Hey, Frank, what do we want—"

Electrical impulses in Frank's brain cells connect, multiply, form a pattern, make an idea.

"That's it!" says Frank. "Exactly, Watson. What do we want? And we work back from there." Frank starts pacing again. "First, obviously, win the Midville Science Prize. But more importantly—master all science. The word comes from the Latin for *knowledge*. We want *all* science. *All* knowledge. Klink and Klank, your robot brains make this possible."

"Obviously," says Klink.

"Doo-bee-doo-bee-doo," hums Klank.

Frank points to a picture on his Wall of Science. "Like this guy, Aristotle. He wanted the science of everything."

Aristotle

Watson answers, "No—"

"You're right, Watson," says Frank. "It's not about Aristotle. Let's divide all of science into six areas. Then, with Klink and Klank, we study each area, and we learn

MATTER

everything!" Frank pins a symbol to the top left corner of the Wall. "First, *matter*. Atoms, molecules, elements, compounds. States of matter. What atoms are made of—protons, neutrons, electrons. And antimatter."

Watson holds up one hand. "Yeah, but—"

"But what about *energy*?" asks Frank. "Exactly. That's next, Watson." Frank pins a second symbol to the top of the Wall, next to the first. "Energy. It's what makes all life possible. We are alive because energy from the sun is converted into food . . . that we convert back to energy to run everything in our bodies. And there's light, sound, motion, magnetism, electricity—all different kinds of energy. Then there are

ENERGY

Forces, Laws of Motion. All stuff we know from Sir Isaac Newton!"

Klank hears the name Newton and chimes in: **"There once was a fellow named Newton, whose beans gave him trouble with tootin'—"**

"Stop that limerick right there," says Klink. "That is not true."

"So—" begins Watson.

"So what about *humans*? Perfect, Watson. That should be next. Frank pins up a third symbol. "Humans. How the human body works. All its different systems. Bones, blood, nerves, breathing. The brain, organs, senses, all the different kinds of cells . . ."

"No," says Watson, showing the paper in his hand. "I mean we should—"

"Go bigger! Study *life*! All living things!" Frank throws up his hands and paces around the workbench. He pins up a fourth paper. "Life. Of course—the next logical step. The interconnections of plants, animals, and people. How everything fits into the bigger picture. How we organize and classify all living things. Reptiles, mammals, birds, and bees ..."

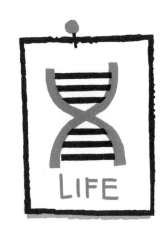

"Animal, Plant, Fungi, Protist," Klink chants.

Watson squints at the Wall of Science. "Wow. I gotta tell you, I—"

"I'm amazed, too." Frank rubs his hands together. "So

much. So incredible. And then how all of this works on our planet." Frank pins up a fifth symbol. "Yes, *Earth*. Continents, oceans, climates, weather, types of rocks ..."

Klank lights up. **"Hey, what is a rock's favorite music?"**

"A rock cannot have favorite music. It cannot hear music."

"Rock and roll!" Klank dances to ROCK BEAT 2.

"Ummmmmmm," says Watson, knowing what is coming next.

"Brilliant," answers Frank, pinning the sixth symbol to the top of the Wall. "Everything. The *universe*. Where Earth fits into our solar system. Our galaxy, space, other suns, other planets, maybe even other universes . . ."

Watson holds his head in his hands.

Frank spins around and looks at his charts of dinosaurs, birds, fish, and mammals. He takes in his diagrams of steam engines, lightbulbs, jet engines. He checks his portraits of Galileo, Charles Darwin, Albert Einstein.

"So much science," says Frank. "Almost *too* much."

The tiny DroneBug high above zooms its camera eye in tight on the paper Watson is holding.

"It is *definitely* too much," says Watson. "Because I

just want to know what we want"—he raises the takeout menu he has been holding for the last twenty minutes—"for lunch."

"Oh," says Frank, still thinking about matter, energy, humans, life, Earth, and the universe. "Probably pizza. And most definitely with *everything* on it."

10

WATSON GRABS THE LAST SLICE OF THE BELLYBOMB SUPREME. He spots Frank eyeing him. "What? You want this?"

"No," says Frank. "I am just always amazed that you eat like a horse and look like a beanpole. We are going to have to design an experiment on you when we get to the human body systems."

"Pepperoni, mushrooms, ham, black olives, ground beef, onion, green pepper, sausage, cheese, chicken, spinach, bacon . . . ohhhhhhhh," says Klank.

"No," says Frank. "You are a robot. Do not put anything into your input port again."

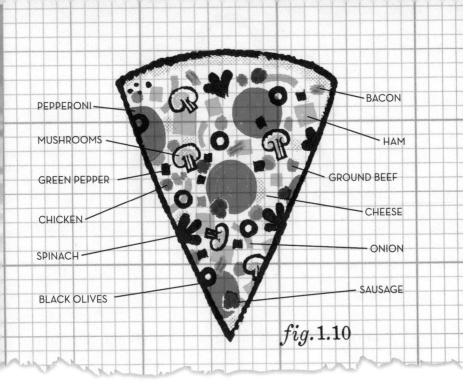

PEPPERONI

MUSHROOMS

GREEN PEPPER

CHICKEN

SPINACH

BLACK OLIVES

BACON

HAM

GROUND BEEF

CHEESE

ONION

SAUSAGE

fig. 1.10

"Dextrose, potassium sorbate, modified corn starch, partially hydrogenated soybean oil, sodium phosphate, citric acid, ferrous gluconate, BHA, BHT," adds Klink. "And yellow number 5."

Frank rolls out his diagrams, charts, and blueprints on the workbench. Klink, Klank, and Watson gather around.

"So, to build the ultimate science-prize project, we start with the first section of our total-science layout—*matter*. The building blocks of everything. This paper, this table, this cardboard pizza box, this pepperoni, this water, the air. Solid, liquid, gas. Everything in the universe is made of matter."

*fig.*1.11

Watson finishes off his slice of BellyBomb Supreme—cheese, crust, yellow number 5 and all. "You sound like a science textbook."

"Exactly correct," says Klink.

"I am hungry," says Klank.

"You cannot be hungry."

"How do you know?"

"You are a robot."

"So are you."

"I know I am."

"Maybe you are not."

"That is ridiculous."

"Yes, you are."

"No, I am not."

"You are not a robot?"

"Aieeeee! *Ding!* In. Three. Hundred. Yards. Turn. Left," Klink intones in his worst GPS voice. "Recalculating." Klink smacks himself in the memory circuits and reboots. "I really wish you would not do that to me."

"Guys!" yells Frank. "Stop it. We don't have time."

"Yes," Klink resumes in his regular voice. "Matter is made of tiny particles called atoms. Atoms are made of even smaller particles called protons, neutrons, and electrons."

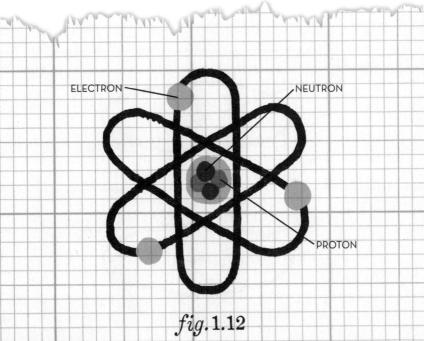

ELECTRON

NEUTRON

PROTON

*fig.*1.12

"Like this pizza is made of dough and cheese and toppings," says Watson.

"Kind of," says Frank.

"So you're going to make a model of an atom?" guesses Watson.

Frank leans over the table. "Watson, please. Any second grader can make a model of an atom. My invention, my project, goes beyond matter—to antimatter."

"Hmmmmm," hums Klink. He quotes, "Antimatter— elementary particles with the mass of ordinary matter, but with the opposite charge."

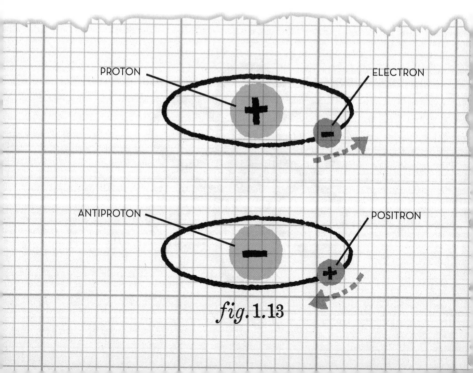

PROTON

ELECTRON

ANTIPROTON

POSITRON

fig. 1.13

Watson frowns. "Ele-who? With what?"

Frank translates Klink's definition. "Scientists believe that for a lot of the small pieces that make up an atom, there are exactly the same pieces with an opposite electrical charge."

"Antiprotons and positrons are the antiparticles of protons and electrons."

"And here's the crazy part: When this antimatter is combined with its matter," continues Frank, "annihilation occurs. And that releases *huge* amounts of energy."

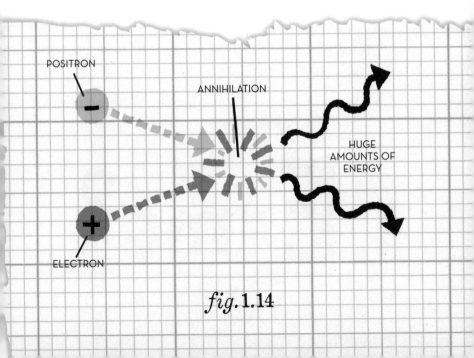

POSITRON

ANNIHILATION

HUGE
AMOUNTS OF
ENERGY

ELECTRON

*fig.*1.14

"Is annihilation delicious?" asks Klank.

"Oh, do not start that again," moans Klink.

"That's actually a good question," says Frank. "Because you are a machine. You need to 'eat' energy to operate. If we can perfect my invention, that's exactly what we can use it for—to 'feed' all the machines in the world."

"But that's nuts," says Watson. "You would need to smash together a lot of matter and antimatter to power all the machines in the world."

Frank smiles. "No, that's the best part. It only takes a teeny bit of matter mixed with the same teeny bit of antimatter to make the biggest amount of energy."

"True," says Klink. "Your other Einstein wrote the equation that calculates the amount of energy from matter exactly."

"*E* equals *mc* squared," says Frank. "The amount of

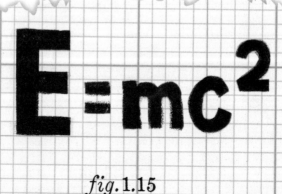

$$E = mc^2$$

fig. 1.15

energy created can be figured out by multiplying the mass of the particle times the speed of light squared."

Frank picks a mushroom off the pizza box. "So if we had this mushroom and its antimushroom . . . Let's say their mass is 1 gram."

Frank types into his calculator.

"The energy created from smashing them together would equal 1 gram times the speed of light squared. What's the speed of light, Klink?"

"300,000 kilometers per second."

"So we square that." Frank calculates, "300,000 times 300,000 equals . . . 90 billion kilometers per second squared. We multiply that times the 1 gram. So from 1 gram of mushroom and antimushroom, we get 90 billion units of pure energy!"

$$\text{Energy} = 1 \times 300,000^2$$
$$\text{Energy} = 1 \times 90,000,000,000$$
$$\text{Energy} = 90 \text{ billion}$$

"I have no idea what you're talking about. But that's a crazy amount of energy from one mushroom!" says Watson.

Frank faces his new robot pals. "Can we combine matter and antimatter?"

Klank nods. **"Does a robot clank in the woods?"**

Klink studies Frank's sketches and drawings. He instantly searches, scans, reads everything he can find on creating and annihilating antimatter.

"It is not impossible." concludes Klink.

"So what would you make with all that energy?" asks Watson.

Frank smiles. "I would make my—"

Frank hears a very faint, very tiny, very mechanical, buglike zzzzzzzzz. "Wait. Did you hear that?"

"Hear what?" answers Watson. "The fish alarm didn't go off."

Frank pauses, looks around, then rolls out his plan.

A KID WEARING SIZE-FIVE WING-TIP SHOES HUNCHES OVER A GIANT polished black desk, staring intently at one of six high-definition video screens. The screen labeled DRONEBUG'S-EYE VIEW.

"Man, I hate this guy!" says the kid. "It's bad enough he invents two great robots. But then all he does with them is talk—'blah, blah, I love science this, blah, blah, I love science that.' What a moron. What an idiot."

"*Eeeep, meep,*" replies the chimpanzee in the pin-striped pants sitting at the controls next to the kid.

The big robot on the screen says, **"Does a robot clank in the woods?"**

"What did he say?"

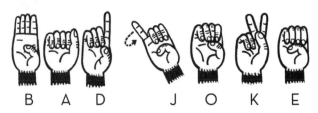

B A D   J O K E

Edison—because yes, of course it is T. Edison in his headquarters, because really, who else wears size-five wing-tip shoes?—looks even more closely.

"Those robots are going to be tough to beat for the Science Prize. But Frank Einstein is not going to one-up me again!" Edison slaps his hand on the desk. "Wait. What is that? They are making plans for something else. Zoom in!"

T O O   N O I S Y

"Don't tell me it's too noisy, you pooping primate. Zoom in!"

Mr. Chimp toggles the joystick control on the master panel. The picture zooms in tight on Frank Einstein.

On the screen, Frank pauses. "Wait. Did you hear that?"

Mr. Chimp leans back in his office chair. He crosses his big, hairy bare feet on the desk. He pulls out the small metal antbox from his pants pocket and pushes a slender stick into the hole on top.

"Hear what?" answers Watson on-screen. "The fish alarm didn't go off."

Mr. Chimp pulls out the ant-covered stick and licks up a quick snack.

On the DRONEBUG'S-EYE VIEW screen, Frank Einstein pauses, then rolls out his plan.

"I can't believe this," says Edison. "Is that what I think it is?"

Mr. Chimp tucks his antbox back in his pocket, brushing a few stray ant legs off his white shirt and striped tie.

"No!" screams Edison. "No, no, no!" He thrashes around in a tantrum, scattering papers, knocking pens and pencils flying.

Mr. Chimp grabs the joystick with his toes and scans the DroneBug camera over the plans. He signs:

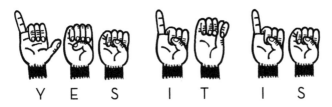

"Yes, I know it *is* what I think it is, you mangy monkey! But, no, *this cannot happen*! That goober Einstein cannot win the Science Prize!"

Mr. Chimp curls back his lips and shows his teeth again in what a human might think was a smile. But if you were a chimpanzee, you would know Mr. Chimp was thinking about biting your throat out, ripping your arm off, and beating you senseless with it.

"So Einstein has a plan?" says Edison. "Well, I have a plan, too. Mr. Chimp, listen up!"

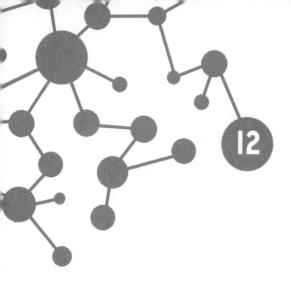

12

LINK, KLANK, FRANK, AND WATSON KICK INTO HIGH GEAR.

Frank lays out his wrenches and soldering iron, screwdrivers and pliers, hacksaw and hammer, rulers, clamps, and files.

He consults his plan and directs his team.

Klink prints out blueprints, charts, and formulas.

Klank hauls in bits and pieces of a bicycle, mower, and motorcycle—wires, tires, chains, and gears—from the yard.

Watson raids the repair shop and the kitchen for nuts and bolts and corkscrews and magnets.

Frank solders and connects, screws and bolts, ham-

mers and files. Klink and Frank check, test, recheck and retest, and test some more.

Time flies by without anyone noticing it.

Until suddenly the fish on the wall wiggles, flips its head sideways, and starts singing, "WE ARE THE CHAMPIONS! WE ARE THE CHAMPIONS!"

"Everyone under the workbench!" calls Frank. "No one can know about you guys or our project yet."

Watson throws a blue tarp over everything and dives under the workbench with Klink and Klank.

"Move over," beeps Klank. **"You are hogging all the room."**

"I am not." whispers Klink.

"Stop pushing," hisses Watson.

"Shhhhhhhh!" says Frank, just as the door to the lab opens and—

"Hello, scientists!"

Watson, pushed by Klank's big foot, rolls out from under the workbench. "Oh, hi, Grampa Al."

"Dr. Watson! Good to see you . . . uh, playing with the new robots?"

Watson jumps to his feet. "Oh, no. We are working on

Science Prize stuff here. I've perfected my Peanut Butter Bubble Gum. And just wait till you see what Frank has."

Klink and Klank roll, crawl, and unpack themselves from under the workbench.

"Hey, boys. Good to see you again. What have you been up to all morning?"

Klank hums, blinks his antenna, and answers, **"I have been up to about 1.8288 meters all morning. Or, in American measurements, six feet."**

"Ha! Good one," laughs Grampa Al.

"Except he's not kidding," says Frank. "He means it."

Klink revs his vacuum engine. **"We have actually been combining atoms and anti-atoms to produce energy for Frank Einstein's invention."**

"Ha! Another good one. Making your own particle collider. Just like my scientist pals at CERN, who have been smashing atomic parts together for years and spending millions of dollars to do it." Grampa Al winks at Watson. "And you guys did it all in one day. With repair-shop junk. You robots are funnier than a monkey's uncle."

"He's not kidding either." Frank whips the blue tarp

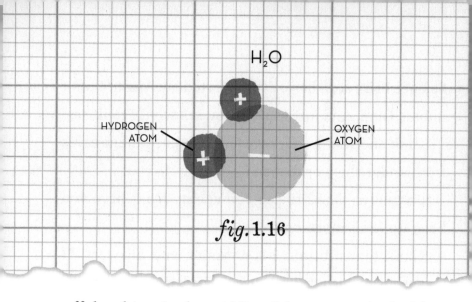

fig. 1.16

off the object in the middle of the room. It looks like a bike from the future. Instead of pedals and gears, it has a small silver motor.

Grampa Al checks it out and nods. "Your flying bicycle. I remember when you were working on this."

"But I could never get enough power in a small-enough engine."

Grampa Al looks more closely at the engine, and his eyes go wide. "No! Really? So you mean you and your robots made an—"

"Antimatter Motor," says Frank.

Grampa Al takes off his faded NASA baseball cap and whistles. "Well, if that isn't the bee's knees. Unbelievable!"

"Oh, very believable," says Klink. "A small amount

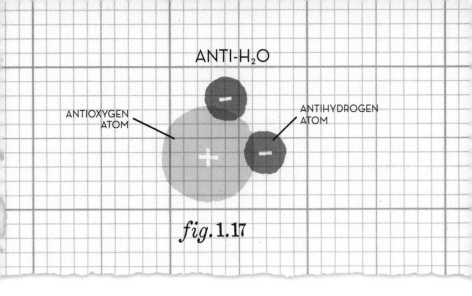

ANTI-H$_2$O

fig. 1.17

of H$_2$O combined with an equal amount of anti-H$_2$O produces—"

"Crazy amounts of energy!" marvels Grampa Al.

Frank holds up an eyedropper. "You are just in time for the first test run. We have the antiwater we made all loaded. All we need to add now is the one drop of water."

Grampa Al puts a hand on Frank's arm. "Frank, this is really dangerous."

"Don't worry, Grampa. We've run all our tests. We've double-checked everything. The Antimatter Motor Fly Bike is good."

"One hundred percent. All systems go," Klink reports.

"Boom-chicka-boom-chicka-boom," TECHNO-BEATS Klank.

Grampa Al nods. "It's not your Fly Bike I'm worried about. It's what other people might do with your anti-matter invention if they get ahold of it."

"No one else can do this," says Frank, "because no one else has Klink and Klank. And isn't this just the coolest bike ever?"

Grampa Al scratches his head and smiles. "Absolutely cool."

"This is going to work, Grampa," Frank says. "The Antimatter Motor Fly Bike is going to win the prize, and we are going to keep this place forever."

Grampa Al smiles and nods.

Frank carries the Antimatter Motor Fly Bike out into the deserted alley and empty lot behind Grampa Al's building. He loads the motor with one drop of water to mix with the one drop of antiwater. He straps his helmet on tight, hops on the bike, and with one small flick of his thumb on the ignition switch, fires up the most amazing invention, powered by the smallest bit of matter meeting the smallest bit of antimatter with a powerful *HMMMMMMMMMM*.

The Fly Bike rises easily off the ground. Frank guns

it forward with a lean and a twist of the acceleration handgrip.

"Oh yeah!" cheers Watson.

Frank jets a quick circle down the alley and back. He banks a faster figure eight in the empty lot. He jumps the broken couch, flips over the stack of empty milk crates, goes horizontal along the back wall of the shop building, and does a nosedive 360, spinning to a stop exactly seven centimeters from Watson's left toe.

Klink nods his webcam eye. "Energy from matter."

Klank gives Frank a one-arm hug. **"Sweet moves."**

Watson slides his toe back, just a bit. "An Antimatter Motor Fly Bike *and* Watson's Universal-Strength Peanut Butter Bubble Gum? Tomorrow that Science Prize is ours for sure."

Frank guns the Antimatter Motor with another deep *HMMMMMMM.*

Which might be why no one hears, or sees, a tiny metal bug fly up and out of Frank Einstein's lab.

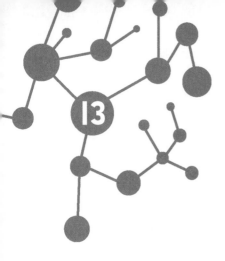

13

OOD MORNING, EINSTEIN," SAYS GRAMPA AL, POURING FRANK some cornflakes.

Frank plops down in the kitchen chair and yawns but still cracks a smile and answers, "Good morning, Einstein."

"Cornflakes!" says Watson, already there and ready to go, as loud and awake as Frank is not. He holds a single cornflake up to the light. "This is what I am going to invent next."

Frank chews his mouthful of cereal. Sleepily. Slowly. "I think they've already been invented."

"No, I mean something *like* cornflakes. Something

that is such a good idea that it seems like it's always been around. Did you know they were invented by accident?"

"No," says Frank. "But why do I have a feeling you're going to tell me anyway?"

"It's 1894," says Watson, ignoring Frank. "The Kellogg brothers are making some dough to squeeze through rollers and flatten out. But then they both have to leave the room for some reason. I'm not sure why. Maybe their mom is calling them. No . . . wait. They were grown-up guys by then. I guess it's not part of the story—"

"Which is why you should probably leave it out," says Frank.

"Right," says Watson. "Forget that part. So they have to leave the room. They come back. And guess what? The dough is all dried out. They don't want to waste it, though, so they run it through the rollers anyway."

"OK, now this is getting really exciting," teases Frank.

"But when they run the dry dough through the rollers, it breaks into flakes! They are delicious. Everyone loves them. And now they've been around for more than a hundred years."

"Which just might happen with Watson's Universal-

Strength Peanut Butter Bubble Gum," says Grampa Al. He checks his full-scale model of the first atomic clock on the kitchen wall.

"Speaking of which—we'd better get you boys over to City Hall so you can get set up. Big day today."

The thought of today's Science Prize, and the Anti-matter Motor Fly Bike—what it could mean for Grampa Al, what it could mean for science—wakes Frank up in an instant. But—

Rrrrarrrrrr rings the Dimetrodon.

Frank answers. "Hey, Mom. Hey, Dad."

Bob and Mary Einstein, still in their orange parkas, appear on the Dimetrodon screen.

"Hi, darling. We can't talk long. There is something happening down here with that orange zone you mentioned."

"It's the ozone, honey," says Bob.

"Right. The O zone. Seems like it's got a hole in it."

"Yeah, there's a bad thing going on with CFCs . . ." Frank begins to explain patiently.

"Yes, but *any*way. We just wanted to call and wish you luck at your science fair today."

"Aw, thanks, Mom. I'm hoping to win the big prize. Remember the trophy Grampa won when he was a kid?"

"Did you do that model of a volcano with flour and seltzer like I did when I was your age?" asks Bob. "That's a classic."

"Not exactly," says Frank. "It's baking soda and vinegar. And they do react in a pretty neat multistep reaction to form carbonic acid . . .

$$NaHCO_3 + HC_2H_3O_2 \rightarrow NaC_2H_3O_2 + \mathbf{H_2CO_3}$$

". . . which decomposes into water and bubbles of carbon dioxide . . .

$$H_2CO_3 \rightarrow \mathbf{H_2O} + \mathbf{CO_2}$$

". . . but actually, I finally figured out how to power my old flying-bike invention. With a real Antimatter Motor I made with Watson and my robot pals."

The picture link fuzzes for a split second.

"What?" says Mary. "We didn't hear all of that. But it's

wonderful that you are riding bikes with your friends."

"We are heading home tomorrow," says Bob. "See you in a couple days!"

"Love you, sweetie."

"Love you guys. Bye."

Frank turns to Grampa Al. "You let your own kid make a volcano model?"

Grampa Al smiles and shrugs. "He loved it. And it made a very nice imitation-lava flow. Now come on. Pack up your Fly Bike and Peanut Butter Bubble Gum, and let's blow this pop stand."

"Blow this pop stand" is another one of those mysterious Grampa Al sayings, where you know what he means but you really have no idea what he just said.

Frank jumps up and hustles to his laboratory.

"I've got my Peanut Butter Bubble Gum right here and all ready to go," says Watson. "Want another piece?"

"Maybe later. I'm still trying to unstick my right molars," says Grampa Al. "But hey, on second thought, it might be just what I need." He pulls his bongo drum out from under the table and smooths a piece of Watson's Universal-Strength Gum into a crack in the wood. Grampa Al plays a quick couple of beats and gives Watson a thumbs-up for his invention.

Frank flings open the door to the lab. "Time to fly!" He pulls the blue tarp off the Antimatter Motor Fly Bike.

"OK, Klink and Klank, we are antimatter-flying out of here. We'll be back in a couple hours . . . with the Midville Science Prize trophy and the cash."

Frank waits for a second to hear a sarcastic crack from Klink and a bad joke from Klank.

But there is nothing.

"Klink? Klank?" Frank looks around the lab. It suddenly seems very empty.

Frank leans the Antimatter Motor Fly Bike against the wall and looks out into the yard and junk pile.

"Klink! Klank!"

Nothing.

No one.

No robots.

Frank instantly knows that something is seriously wrong. Klink and Klank did not just step out for what Grampa Al would call a "constitutional."

Frank hurries back inside and examines the whole lab for a clue.

Nothing.

No, wait. There on the paper plans. Small black specks. Dirt? Pepper? Frank wets a finger, picks a piece up, and looks more closely. "It's some kind of insect leg."

Who would leave an insect leg behind? And why?

Frank crushes the disembodied leg between his fingers

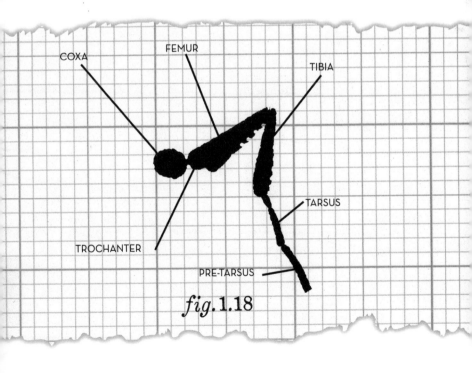

fig. 1.18

and smells it. A sharp, acid, chemical scent, like really intense Magic Marker, fills his nose.

"Frank! Come on, let's go!" Watson calls from the kitchen door.

Frank drops the insect leg. He carries his Antimatter Motor Fly Bike into the kitchen and gives Grampa Al and Watson the bad news.

"Klink and Klank have been robot-napped!"

14

THE FIX IT! TRUCK SPEEDS THROUGH THE SLOW-MORNING-TRAFFIC streets of Midville, taking corners tight, drifting wide on the turns, and roaring full-throttle down straightaways.

Watson wraps his arms around his Universal-Strength Peanut Butter Bubble Gum boxes. He wonders out loud, "Should that light on the dashboard be blinking red?"

Grampa Al gives his

gauges a quick glance as he leans into the next turn. "Oh yeah," he says. "This engine likes to run hot. It's a regulation NASCAR 850 horsepower V-8. We are talking—"

Squeeeeeeeeaaallll! whine the truck tires on the turn.

"—around two thousand degrees Fahrenheit. Just like I used to run in my stock-car-racing days."

"You never told me you used to race stock cars," says Frank, surprised once again by something he doesn't know about his Grampa Al.

Grampa Al smiles. "You never asked." He passes two cars on the Oak Street straightaway, downshifts into an S-turn, and passes two more cars coming out high. "But hey, are you sure you don't want to look for Klink and Klank now? You don't have to do this Science Prize for me."

"I'm sure," says Frank, grabbing the door handle as Grampa Al brakes hard and fishtails ninety degrees right on Main Street. "I am going to win this prize. Then we can look for Klink and Klank. If you can get us there on time."

Grampa Al checks his navy dive watch and gives Frank a nod. "Roger that. And while you guys are in there kicking butt, I will get started looking for Klink and Klank."

Grampa Al floors it past the Midville Cemetery, blows by the courthouse plaza, and weaves around a gold mini-van, a blue station wagon, and a poky red pickup truck. Still going full speed, he yanks up the emergency brake and pulls the steering wheel hard left. The truck locks all four wheels and skids sideways to a full stop, perfectly curbside, right in front of City Hall. Tires smoking just a little bit.

"Hit the beach, guys!"

Frank and Watson pile out of the truck. Watson lugs his boxes of gum and poster-board display. Frank grabs his ultralight Antimatter Motor Fly Bike. Together they race up the wide stadium steps of the white-marbled and many-columned City Hall building into a swarm of kids carrying working-eye models, prime-number charts, fruit-fly genetics displays, blown-up earthworm dissections, a poster of photon and positron emissions from a black hole, solar panels, optical illusions, and, yes, baking-soda volcanoes.

The herd of one hundred kid scientists pours into the high-ceilinged cavern of the main hall under the enormous banner of the sponsor, GrabCo. Each scientist checks in with GrabCo officials, receives a GRABCO SCIENCE PRIZE

CONTESTANT badge, and is directed to a numbered spot in the maze of tables filling the patterned marble floor.

The packed main hall hums like some kind of gargantuan beehive filled with a swarm of kid-size buzzing bees setting up, comparing projects, talking science.

In spot 338B, Watson arranges the finishing touch, the final piece of his Universal-Strength Peanut Butter Bubble Gum, on a very attractive pyramid display.

In spot 403A, Frank Einstein adjusts his Antimatter Motor Fly Bike diagram.

And that's when the lights suddenly go out.

A surprised hush quiets the roaring buzz.

A squeal of feedback echoes around the hall.

A single spotlight pops on a raised stage, illuminating two men in bow-tied tuxedoes.

A voice booms, "LADY AND GENTLEMAN SCIENTISTS. WELCOME TO THE FIFTIETH ANNUAL GRABCO SCIENCE PRIZE. I AM ADAMS JOHNSON, PRESIDENT OF GRABCO, AND WE HAVE A SURPRISE ANNOUNCEMENT. PROBABLY THE BIGGEST SURPRISE WE HAVE EVER HAD IN OUR FIFTY YEARS

OF AWARDING THE GRABCO SCIENCE PRIZE. MR. MAYOR?"

The one tuxedoed man gives the microphone to the other.

"AHHHEM!" The mayor coughs nervously into the mic. "WE, UH . . . WELL, AH . . . HAVE THIS ANNOUNCE-MENT . . ." Someone says something to the mayor. "OH, YES. I AM MR. MAYOR. ALSO THE MAYOR OF MID-VILLE. SO YOU CAN CALL ME MAYOR MAYOR. HA-HA."

No one, except GrabCo president Adams Johnson, laughs. Everyone has heard this from Mayor Mayor before. And it is never funny.

"WELL, OK, THEN . . . THIS MORNING WE GOT TO SEE AN INVENTION SO AMAZING . . . WE ARE SO SURE IT IS GOING TO CHANGE THE WORLD . . . THAT WE, UH . . . JUST HAD TO, AH . . . AWARD THE SCIENCE PRIZE THIS YEAR, WITHOUT EVEN SEE-ING ANY OF THE OTHER ENTRIES, TO THIS YOUNG MAN . . . T. EDISON!"

The assembled crowd gasps in surprise.

A kid in an old-fashioned coat and tie steps into the

spotlight and grabs the microphone. He speaks quickly to drown out the rising protests and boos.

"THANK YOU SO MUCH, MAYOR MAYOR AND GRABCO PRESIDENT MR. JOHNSON. I WANT TO CONGRATULATE ALL YOU BUDDING SCIENTISTS FOR BEING HERE. BUT I REALLY HAVE CREATED THE BEST INVENTION EVER—"

"That stinks!" someone yells.

Edison speeds quickly to his point.

"A MOTOR THAT COMBINES MATTER AND ANTI-MATTER AND PRODUCES ALMOST UNLIMITED EN-ERGY FROM A SINGLE DROP OF WATER!"

Across the rows of science projects, Frank Einstein and Watson lock eyes.

"No," says Frank to no one in particular, but to the whole world at large.

"Boooo!" yells a voice in the crowd.

"That's not fair!" yells another voice.

"Prove it!" yells another.

A small, powerful, hairy figure in pin-striped pants and bare feet walks to the edge of the stage, stares out into the crowd, and appears to smile. It is Mr. Chimp.

Mr. Chimp walks to one side of the stage and pulls on a gold tasseled rope. The red curtains behind him swoosh open and display a small, brightly lit silver motor on a pedestal. Next to it lies what looks like the prong end of the biggest extension cord in the world.

"WITH THIS ONE DROP OF WATER," Edison booms over the noise of the restless crowd, "I WILL SUPPLY POWER TO ALL OF MIDVILLE FOR THE ENTIRE YEAR. FOR FREE!"

The murmurings of the crowd turn a bit brighter.

"AND . . . AND . . . SINCE I AM SUCH A NICE GUY, I WILL SHARE MY ONE-HUNDRED-THOUSAND-DOLLAR GRABCO SCIENCE PRIZE . . . WITH EV-ERYONE HERE. GIVING EVERY ONE OF YOU—MY FELLOW SCIENTISTS—ONE THOUSAND DOLLARS EACH!"

Now the crowd outright cheers.

"No, no, no," says Frank Einstein.

Edison makes a big show of walking over to the silver machine and placing a single drop of water into its fuel tank.

"MR. CHIMP, PLUG IN ALL OF MIDVILLE POWER AND LIGHT. LET THE FREE ENERGY FLOW. AND, FELLOW SCIENTISTS, TELL EVERYONE YOU KNOW THAT YOU HAVE SEEN THE WONDER OF . . . THE EDISON ANTIMATTER MOTOR!"

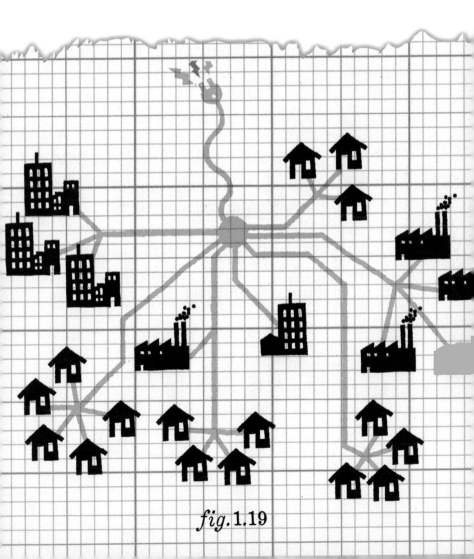

*fig.*1.19

Mr. Chimp inserts the massive plug into the socket connected to the Edison Antimatter Motor. The lights in the great hall blaze back on.

The national anthem blares from every speaker.

Parachute-size red, white, and blue banners unfurl from the ceiling.

A forty-foot bank of LED lights covering one wall blinks alternately:

FREE, SAFE, AND CLEAN ENERGY

THE EDISON ANTIMATTER MOTOR

Now the crowd (all but two) goes completely crazy. Someone on stage, actually Edison himself, starts a chant in a poorly disguised voice. "Ed-i-son, Ed-i–son, Ed-i-son.

"ONE THOUSAND DOLLARS FOR EVERY KID HERE," Edison reminds the crowd. "AND DON'T FOR-GET TO PICK UP YOUR GRABCO SCIENCE PRIZE

CERTIFICATE OF PARTICIPATION. Ed-i-son, Ed-i-son, Ed-i-son . . ."

The Midville Science Prize contestants surge happily toward the stage to get their payoff, and join the chant. "Ed-i-son, Ed-i-son, Ed-i-son . . ."

They are curling back their lips and showing a lot of teeth.

This worries Mr. Chimp.

Frank lifts his Antimatter Motor Fly Bike onto his display table to avoid getting swept forward by the waves of kids flooding toward the stage. He looks for Watson. But even Watson is gone. Heading for the stage? And his thousand dollars?

Frank Einstein straddles his bike and fires up its Anti-Matter Motor with the touch of a single button. He looks over his shoulder in disgust at the cheering crowd still chanting Edison's name. He leans forward and zooms off above the tables, over the risers, and right through the MIDVILLE, A LOVELY PLACE stained-glass window with a sharp crash and a shattering of glass that almost no one even hears or sees.

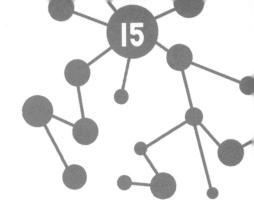

15

O N THE SANDY GROUND AT THE TOP OF THE HIGHEST HILL UNDER the oldest oak tree in the Midville Forest Preserve, the last wave of the red-ant army attacks the entrance to the black ants' hill. A line of giant-headed black soldier ants meet and mow down the charge, easily chopping the red ants to pieces with their jagged, oversized mandibles.

The invading red-ant army is reduced to a scattering of heads, abdomens, and thorax parts, bent feelers, and ripped-off legs.

The black-ant army is victorious.

A speck appears in the blue sky near the horizon.

The speck grows larger. The speck takes the shape of a bike flying above the ground, carrying a hunched-over figure. The flying bike zooms into full-size close-up, banks around the oak tree, and drops suddenly and quickly to the ground right next to the black ants' hill.

One large sneaker-covered foot swings over the bike and down, right on top of the band of black soldier ants, smashing two flat and scattering the rest.

The kid wearing the sneaker sits down on the slate rock under the oak tree, folds his arms across his chest, and stares out over the whole town of Midville spread below, thinking a thousand thoughts, electrical impulses in his brain jumping from neuron to neuron, oblivious to the ant chaos he has just caused under his rubber-tipped toe.

Frank Einstein—because, really, who else drives a flying bike?—thinks.

The Earth revolves. Time passes. Frank feels flattened. Like he has been stomped by a giant shoe. The ants next to Frank's sneaker begin digging a new tunnel, begin mounding a new anthill.

Frank mutters darkly to himself, "'Best invention ever . . . Single drop of water . . . The *Edison Antimatter Motor* . . .'"

Frank forms thoughts of smashing, breaking, throwing everything away.

The Earth revolves.

Frank mutters more. "Even Watson . . . Robots lost . . . Oh no, Grampa Al—"

"At your service."

Frank looks up to see Grampa Al, who has just stepped out from around the oak.

"Huh? How . . . ? What are you doing here?"

Grampa Al slings off a small rucksack and sits down on the rock next to Frank.

"I heard about the Science Prize. And I didn't have any luck tracking down Klink and Klank. So I thought I might just hike up here and take in this great view."

Frank looks out over Midville. "Nothing great about it

today. Everything is wrecked. What a disaster."

Grampa Al hands Frank his canteen. "Oh, I don't know. It's pretty much the same world it was yesterday. Sun still shining, oak leaves still working their photosynthesis, these ants right under us still digging and hauling."

Frank takes a long swig of water. It does taste good.

"But the Science Prize, Klink and Klank, your shop, your place . . ."

"Ahhhh, none of that's a big deal. You've still got that Frank Einstein brain of yours, right?"

"Yeah."

"You're still Frank Einstein, right?"

"Yeah."

"So you can keep asking questions and finding your own answers. We don't

need trophies or prizes to do that. We are scientists."

Frank looks down at his sneakers. He sees a familiar-looking shape—an insect leg. Just like the one he found in his lab.

Frank picks up the leg, crushes it between thumb and finger, and sniffs a familiar sharp Magic Marker scent.

"Right?" says Grampa Al.

Suddenly everything falls into place.

Frank looks up. In his mind he connects the insect leg, the kidnapping of the robots, the Antimatter Motor . . .

"Ant leg," says Frank. "Ant leg—Mr. Chimp—Edison. That's it!"

"Of course it is." Grampa Al leans back and takes in the view. "Glad we could have this little chat."

"I know *who* kidnapped Klink and Klank. I know *how* Edison got that Antimatter Motor. I know *where* to go next. And I know *what* to do next."

"Then what are you waiting for, Frank Einstein? Shake a leg."

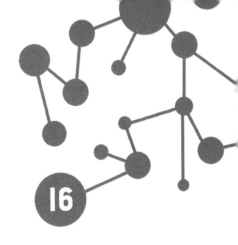

16

SO WHERE ARE KLINK AND KLANK?" ASKS WATSON.

"Here," says Frank, pointing to a spot on the Midville map hastily pinned above the work-bench. He makes a red *X* over the outline of a single building at the southern edge of Midville, right next to Lake Genevieve.

"And smelling a crushed ant leg told you this how . . . ?"

"No time to explain everything, Watson. But I am glad you didn't fall for that Edison pitch—"

"Aw, come on, Frank. You know I'm a better friend than that. I got trampled, and I always freak out when—"

"OK, OK. Good to know," Frank interrupts. "But what

all this means is we need to get to Edison's place. Now. Before he realizes he should destroy the evidence."

Watson smiles. "Good to know" is probably the nicest thing Frank has ever said about their friendship. He would like to hear more, but Frank is already busy marking a flurry of *X*'s on the Midville map, seemingly at random.

"What do you see?" Frank quizzes him.

"I see that you marked up my dad's map that I told him I would take care of, and that now I'm already in trouble and we haven't even left your lab."

"Connect the dots," says Frank. "All the properties that Edison's family has bought up over the past year . . . and kicked people out of . . . and this building, Grampa Al's . . ." Frank connects the *X*'s.

"A big red circle? So Edison is building a racetrack? A gigantic doughnut oven? I don't get it."

Frank puts up another map right below the Midville map. It has an almost identical circle on it.

"A map of CERN, the subatomic-particle physics lab buried under Switzerland and France. It's that place Grampa Al was telling us about, where some of his scientist pals

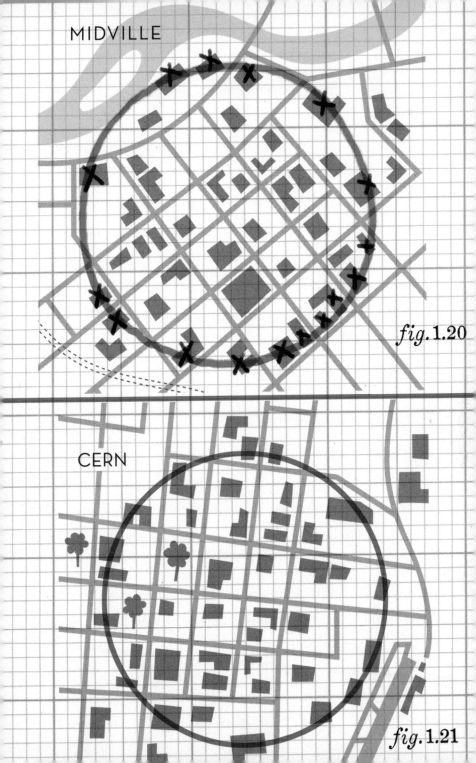

MIDVILLE

fig. 1.20

CERN

fig. 1.21

work. The ring is part of a machine called the Large Hadron Collider."

"Right," says Watson. "Now I really have no idea what you're talking about."

"It's the coolest thing," says Frank. "A seventeen-mile ring that speeds up subatomic particles to almost the speed of light and then smashes them together! Like racing two really, really small cars around a huge racetrack in opposite directions . . . and then smacking them perfectly head-on."

"Really?"

"Really."

"Why?"

"Why?" Frank points to the *matter* section on his Wall of Science. "To record what happens after the collisions and uncover the true nature of matter . . . and antimatter. Think of it as figuring out how those two really little race cars were built by looking at the pieces that come out after the crash."

Watson scratches his head and nods. "So Edison has been secretly building his own collider ring thing and trying to make antimatter all along?"

"Exactly, Watson! And yesterday he somehow found

out that I beat him to it. So last night he had Mr. Chimp robot-nap Klink and Klank so he could steal the secret of my Antimatter Motor from them."

"Wow," says Watson.

"So Edison is likely in this building"—Frank stabs an index finger at the Midville map—"right next to Lake Genevieve, for the water supply he needs to cool all the subatomic reactions. And he's probably hiding Klink and Klank there, too."

Watson jumps up. "Oh, we know that building. It's the Big Black Cube. But that thing is built like a fortress! How are we ever going to get in there?"

Frank studies the two maps. "May I please have a stick of your gum, Watson?"

"Sure! I have plenty. I couldn't even give it away at City Hall. Here, take two or three."

Frank takes one stick of gum and tucks it carefully in his inner lab-coat pocket. "One should be just fine."

"And what does any of this have to do with ant legs?"

"More later," says Frank, motioning Watson toward the door. "Right now we have to be quick . . . and inconspicuous. Let's roll."

17

FRANK AND WATSON ROLL, QUICKLY AND inconspicuously, on their regular bikes, through downtown Midville, across South Midville, and out to the lake.

They skid to a stop in a deserted lot right next to exactly what Watson described—a big black cube. And just as Frank predicted, the building is topped with two lake water-fed cooling towers.

"Ditch the bikes here," says Frank.

They hide both bikes behind a mound of brick and lumber and dirt rubble and approach the Big Black Cube.

There is nothing around the Cube. No fences keeping anyone out. No kennels hiding guard dogs. No towers with floodlights and security guards. Nothing but a bare lot. But it is a fortress because there are no visible doors, vents, or openings of any other kind in the smooth, gunmetal-black surface. The only break in the exterior is a band of windows too high to reach or to see in through.

"So how do we sneak in?" whispers Watson. "Did you secretly copy Edison's fingerprints off a glass you made him pick up back in the shop, and we're going to fool a thumb scanner?"

"Nope."

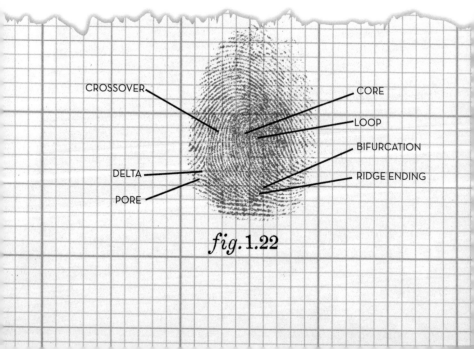

CROSSOVER

CORE

LOOP

BIFURCATION

DELTA

RIDGE ENDING

PORE

fig. 1.22

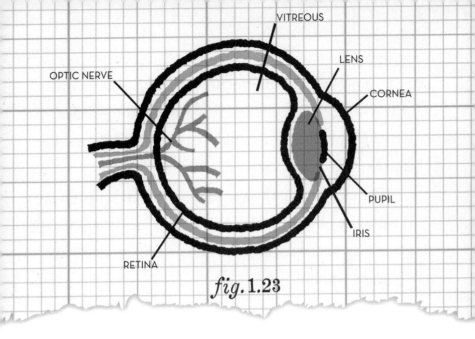

fig.1.23

"You reconstructed his eyeball from a 3-D camera, and we're going to fake out a retina scanner?"

"Nope."

"Tiny portable missile launcher? Giant trained tunneling moles?"

"Nope and nope." Frank scans the ground in front of him carefully. "We need the densest rock we can find. A nice metamorphic or basic igneous would be fine . . ."

Watson picks up a baseball-size piece of speckled black, gray, and reddish rock and shows it to Frank.

Frank hefts it in one hand. "Granite. Perfect."

"So now we grind the granite into dust," guesses Watson, still whispering, "combine it with another powder you have in your lab coat to make instant dynamite, and light it to explode a hole in the side of the Cube?"

"Simpler than that," says Frank. He winds up, pitches the granite chunk at one high window, and smashes the glass with a resounding *crash!*

Sirens whoop.

Lights flash.

Video cameras pop up out of the ground, recording two nearly invisible door panels sliding open and a small army of gray-uniformed security guards running out, grabbing Einstein and Watson, and hustling them inside the Cube.

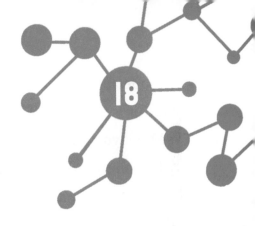

18

WELL, HELLO!" SAYS T. EDISON FROM BEHIND HIS HUGE polished black desk. "What not-a-surprise to see you, Bert and Ernie. I'm sure you are here to congratulate me on my new invention, the Edison Antimatter Motor, yes?"

Mr. Chimp, sitting just to the right of Edison, signs:

Y   E   S

"Hardly," says Frank Einstein. "We are here for some answers."

"Wonderful. What are your questions?"

Watson scans the office. "Why do you have so many TVs? I bet you are spying on people. Like us!"

"Mr. Chimp and I like to watch cartoons. Lots of them. All at the same time. Next question!"

Frank walks around the office, counting his steps and measuring the room's exact dimensions. He checks the door. He notes the heating and air-conditioning vents. He listens to everything. He hears the deep hum of machinery behind the office doors. He leans against a wall and hears a very faint rumba beat. He watches Mr. Chimp take out a small metal box, dip his stick-tool into it, and slurp a quick snack. A few ant legs drop on the desk. Now Frank is sure.

"Where are Klink and Klank?"

Edison raises his eyebrows in surprise. "What's a klink and a klank?"

"My robots," says Frank without raising his voice.

Frank pictures jumping over the desk, screaming at Edison, and slapping the goofy look right off his face. But then he pictures Mr. Chimp, with 98 percent of the same

DNA but five times the strength of anyone fighting in the WWE, tossing him around and snapping most of the bones in his body without even breaking a chimp sweat.

Frank takes the stick of gum out of his lab-coat pocket and calmly chews it.

"The smart robots you robot-napped from Frank's lab," says Watson, leaning threateningly over Edison's desk.

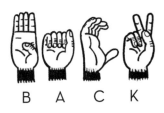

B A C K

Mr. Chimp signs, adding a short, barking "Hroo!" that needs no translation.

"Smart robots, you say? How interesting. You two are quite the Pinky and the Brain. Or maybe Goofus and Gallant?"

Watson backs away from the desk, but he can't take it anymore. "You stole the idea of Frank's Antimatter Motor! You are wrecking our town to build a thing that collides atomic particles! Where are you hiding Klink and Klank?!"

Mr. Chimp looks from Watson to Edison, points one finger at his temple, and moves it in a circle.

Edison laughs.

"Now there's that question again. OK, I guess I might as well tell you." Edison stands up. "A couple of robots did stop by last night. One that looked like a Shop-Vac, and another like a big trash can."

"Yes! That's Klink and Klank!" Watson yells.

"We talked for a bit. Had a nice chat about producing antimatter . . . cheaply. And then I sent them on their way."

"Yeah, right," says Watson. "On their way where?"

"Oh, to a friend's place. I think you and Frank's Grampa Al know him—Junkyard Dog. All the way on the other side of the lake." Edison makes a big deal of checking a brand-new, flashy gold watch. "And they should be having a *smashing* good time . . . right about . . . now. So sorry that you are too late to save them."

"You *what*?" exclaims Frank. "You gave them away to be smashed into scrap metal?"

"Oh, no," says Edison. "I would never do something that crazy. I sold them. Got ten dollars."

Frank grinds his teeth. He clenches his fists. He tenses every muscle. Then he shouts, "NOOOOOOOOO!" and runs right at Edison.

Frank pulls back his fist, leaps over the desk, and is caught in midair by a strong, hairy arm. Watson jumps in, kicking and swinging crazily. Another strong, hairy arm wraps around his waist.

Edison laughs a weird, panting laugh. "Throw them out, Mr. Chimp!"

Frank and Watson struggle and flail and fight against Mr. Chimp.

Watson kicks his legs helplessly in the air. Frank grabs the doorjamb on the way out. But Mr. Chimp doesn't even seem to notice. He tosses Watson first, and then Frank, each a good twenty feet out into the deserted lot.

"Nice visiting with you, Abbott and Costello!" calls Edison from behind Mr. Chimp in the doorway.

Mr. Chimp straightens his tie and seamlessly closes the door of the Big Black Cube with a sticky *shhmmmpp.*

"Owwwwwwww," groans Watson, rolling off a pile of bricks. "Well . . . that went well," he says sarcastically.

Frank stands up, looking strangely not that upset about getting tossed around by a chimpanzee, being called a lot of names, or losing his robot pals.

"Perfectly," Frank says, taking a quick look back at the Cube and brushing off his lab coat.

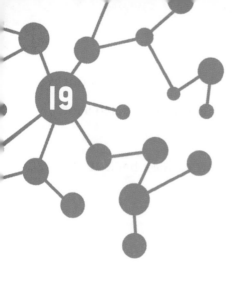

19

"Are you kidding me?"

"I couldn't tell you before, because then you wouldn't have been convincing," says Frank from the passenger seat. "You know you are a terrible actor. And you can't keep a secret."

Watson looks straight ahead. He knows Frank is right. "Well, yeah. So?" Watson sulks.

"But you were amazing in there. You got Edison to talk. And you really whaled on Mr. Chimp. At least for a minute or two."

Watson perks up. "That first karate chop *was* pretty

impressive. So what are we waiting for? Let's go!"

Frank checks the position of the sun in the sky. "Not yet."

Because Frank and Watson aren't going anywhere.

They are not racing across Lake Genevieve at fifty miles per hour, skipping over the choppy waves like Edison thinks they are.

They are not throwing up a rooster tail of spray from the back jet nozzle. They are not peering through the dying light of dusk. They are not running to Junkyard Dog's, hoping they are in time to save Klink and Klank from being smashed into tiny cubes by the car crusher.

They are hiding in a boat, dry-docked on a trailer, just a short walk down the shore from the Big Black Cube.

The setting sun lights up the dramatically cloud-speckled sky in fiery reds and oranges. Frank leans back in his cushioned seat, hands behind his head. "Beautiful, isn't it, Watson?"

Watson and Frank quietly admire the sunset.

"Even more beautiful," Frank continues, "when you know that it's caused by the sunlight rays traveling through more air molecules at sunset. And the short-wavelength blue and green light getting scattered out, leaving the longer-wavelength reds and oranges."

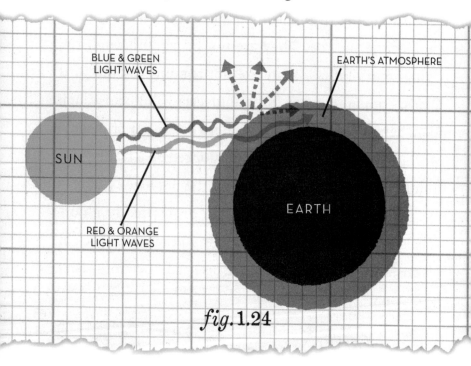

*fig.*1.24

Watson stares at Frank. "Yeah. Just what I *wasn't* thinking."

The last of the sunlight, all wavelengths, disappears.

The darkness of night covers the waterfront. Frank and Watson climb out of their jet-boat hiding place and sneak quickly and quietly back to the side of the Big Black Cube where, not that long ago, they were being tossed out by a chimp.

Frank feels along the smooth side of the Cube. His fingertips find exactly what he is looking for—a small, sticky lump. He pulls out his tiniest, thinnest screwdriver, wedges it in the almost-invisible crack, and eases open a door, its auto-lock mechanism stuck flat and useless by one very sticky wad of Watson's Universal-Strength Peanut Butter Bubble Gum.

Frank motions for Watson to follow him.

Silently they glide down the dimly lit hallway that Frank measured as he was being dragged out. They slip inside an inner door where Frank heard the mechanical and rumba sounds coming from. And they are suddenly inside a gigantic factory filled with massive machines built of magnets and wires and metal panels and computers.

"Whoaaaaa," whispers Watson. "What the heck is this?"

"Just what we thought. Edison's Large Atomic Particle Collider."

"So why did Edison need Klink and Klank and the Antimatter Motor if he has this?"

Frank looks around. "Because my Antimatter Motor is faster and cheaper and better at powering *that*."

Frank points to the far end of the factory, against a brick wall, where the emergency-exit lights outline the shape of what has to be the world's biggest, and most electromagnetic, pink Antimatter Squirt Gun . . .

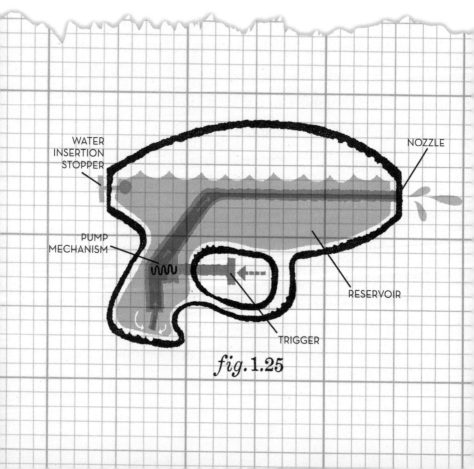

fig. 1.25

. . . powered by a very familiar, small, silver Antimatter Motor.

"Noooooo waaaaay," squeaks Watson.

An access door just to the side of the Antimatter Squirt Gun slides open.

"Shhhhhh. Someone's coming."

Two workers emerge, stepping into the circle of light around the Squirt Gun. The white light reflects off the one worker's glass head and the other worker's metal body.

"Klink!" says Watson.

"And Klank!" says Frank.

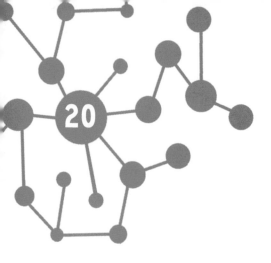

20

WATSON STARTS TO RUN TOWARD THE ROBOTS, BUT FRANK grabs his arm. "Wait! It might be a trap. And I'm sure Edison has more security. Let's watch for a minute."

And, sure enough, in less than a minute, a motorized boom lift wheels around the corner of the particle collider . . . carrying T. Edison and the boom driver, Mr. Chimp.

Frank and Watson duck behind a bank of computers.

"All right, you repair-shop rejects," calls Edison from the boom platform. "Stand over against that wall. Right in front of the target."

"We are hardly rejects," says Klink. "My mental capacity alone is, by any measure, now roughly twelve times that of even your smartest human."

"And you are a robot. And I have decided to get rid of you before that jerk Einstein and his doofus pal—"

"Hey . . ." whispers Watson. "I'm not a doofus."

"—come back snooping around. I will destroy all evidence that you ever helped me. *And* we will get to run the best and final test on the Edison Antimatter Squirt Gun. Win-win!"

Frank and Watson can see Klank's antenna blinking in serious thought.

"But I do not want to be destroyed."

"Hmm," says Edison. "What is Asimov's Second Law of Robotics again?"

Klink beeps, **"A robot must obey orders from humans."**

Edison pushes a remote, and the Edison Antimatter Squirt Gun lights up with a deep hum.

"Great. So I am ordering you two metalheads to get over there in front of that target. Now."

Klink and Klank move slowly along the brick wall and stand in front of the target.

"There is nothing they can do," says Frank. "They can't violate their robot laws. We have to save them."

"Right," says Watson. He jumps up and starts running toward Klink and Klank.

"Though I was thinking we could make a plan first . . ." Frank chases Watson and tries to pull him back, but only manages to catch him just as they both reach a ring of pressure-activated floor plates surrounding the Edison Antimatter Squirt Gun.

The weight of Watson and Frank sinks the floor plate a barely noticeable half inch. But that half inch interrupts a photoelectric light beam, which triggers a

switch, which activates a spring, which shoots a line of titanium bars out of the floor, which trap Watson and Frank in an escape-proof cage against the scarred brick factory wall.

"What?!" yells Edison. And this time he looks truly surprised. "How did you two idiots get in here? You are supposed to be in the junkyard across the lake, saving your robot pals."

Mr. Chimp opens his mouth wide and bares his four large canine teeth.

"Sorry to spoil your test," says Frank. "We just missed you so much, we had to come back and visit again."

Edison uses his remote control to swivel his Edison Antimatter Squirt Gun back and forth. He looks at Klink and Klank.

He looks at Frank and Watson.

He thinks.

He smiles.

"Oh, this is even better. Klink, what is that First Law of Robotics?"

"A robot cannot injure a human, or let a human be injured by not helping."

"Perfect! Now we will get to test the Edison Anti-matter Squirt Gun *and* have Mr. Genius Frank Einstein destroy his own robots. How good is that, Mr. Chimp?"

Mr. Chimp is, for once, actually impressed. He signs:

V E R Y G O O D

Edison fires up his Antimatter Squirt Gun. A stream of white light shoots out of the tip, annihilating all matter in its path on the brick wall. The gun swivels slowly on its base, tracing a line of destruction heading right for Frank and Watson.

"Robots, that antimatter stream is heading right for those two humans. And the only way you can save them is to get in the way of the beam yourselves. Now go!"

Emergency red lights start flashing.

The Danger-Overload siren blares a very loud *whoop-whoop.*

The white-light antimatter beam sizzles across the bricks.

"Don't do it, Klink and Klank!" calls Watson. "Wait What am I saying? I mean, yes, do it! No, wait. Frank! How do we save them *and* us? You do have a plan, right? Tell me you have a plan. Quickly!"

MATTER," SAYS FRANK EINSTEIN, KID GENIUS AND INVENTOR. "The stuff that every living and nonliving thing is made of. That's what this is all about."

"Great," says Frank's longtime pal Watson, crouching behind him. "So how does that help us get out of this?"

Frank Einstein applies, as he always does, the scientific method he learned from his Grampa Al.

Frank thinks:

OBSERVATION:

Red lights flashing twice a second.

Incredibly loud *whoop-whoop* sound echoing over factory floor.

Cage bars: metallic-white color, lightweight, high-strength.

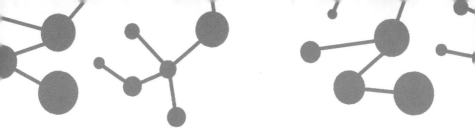

Two mechanical shapes against far brick wall.

Two shadowy figures, both wearing ties, on platform above.

A beam of concentrated white light, sparking and melting a line across near brick wall, presently moving on a path to intersect position of Einstein and Watson in twenty-eight seconds.

Frank says:

"HYPOTHESIS:

"Lights and siren probably an alarm.

"Bars most likely titanium and unbreakable.

"Those two over there might help us.

"Those two up there will not.

"We now have thirteen seconds before every atom, element, molecule, and bit of matter we are made of violently explodes into ashes, heat, and smoke."

"Why do I ever listen to you?" asks Watson, moving as far away as he can from the advancing beam of brick-sizzling light.

Frank Einstein cracks a smile. "Begin **EXPERIMENT** . . ."

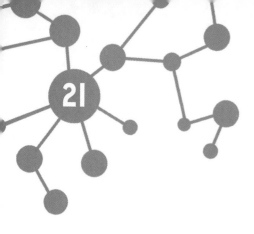

21

IGH UP ON THE BOOM PLATFORM, EDISON STAMPS HIS FEET impatiently. "Come on, you mechanical meatheads! Get your tin butts over there! I want to see some antimatter fireworks!"

"Eeeee-eeee-eee! Ooooo-oooo-ooo!" screams Mr. Chimp, hopping and flapping his arms and kind of losing it, going full chimp for a few wild seconds.

Klink rolls, Klank clomps reluctantly toward their own annihilation.

"I do not want to be antimatter fireworks," whines Klank.

"I told you that humans were unstable thinkers," says Klink. **"What a waste of perfect intelligence—me!"**

The antimatter beam crackles exactly one meter away from the trapped Watson and Frank. Red lights flash. The siren whoops.

As soon as Klink and Klank are close enough to hear him, Frank yells over the deafening siren, "Klank!"

"What?"

"You like to hug, yes?"

"Yes."

"And now you can't hear anything that human on the boom loader says, can you?"

"No."

The antimatter beam now smokes the wall one-half meter away.

Watson covers his eyes.

"Good! So go give that big pink squirt gun the biggest, strongest hug you possibly can. That is a human order!"

Klank thinks for one long, precious second.

Must not let a human be injured. Must obey orders by humans. Frank Einstein orders to hug pink gun. Frank Einstein is human. Hugging gun will not harm a human.

T. Edison can't hear what is happening down below.

But he sees the robots stop. And he knows Einstein is somehow messing with his plans.

Klank's whole metal head lights up with the answer. **"Hug!!!"** He charges the Edison Antimatter Squirt Gun at full, floor-pounding, Klank-stomping speed.

Edison yells at Klank, "Ohdfuhg hwjho ffhjhf dhbhcyy mmrff!"

Or at least that's all Klank hears between the whoops of the siren.

Klank enthusiastically follows Frank's order, smashing into the giant pink pistol with a whanging, full-metal, body-slamming *blllannnnngggg!*

He wraps his big aluminum flex arms around the pistol grip, powers his arm motors to max, punches HEAVY METAL 2, and *squeeeeeze-huuuuuugs* the Edison Antimatter Squirt Gun with every bit of his mechanical strength.

Mr. Chimp sees where this is heading. He lets go of the boom controls and signs:

P E A C E   O U T

Mr. Chimp jumps and grips the top rail with his toes, drops down, and swings his way to safety, hand over foot over hand.

The antimatter beam hits the first titanium bar and vaporizes it.

Frank and Watson back as far away from the bars as they can. Frank recalculates. "OK, that wasn't part of the plan . . ."

"Stop!" yells Edison, at everyone, at everything.

But there is no stopping this antimatter matter.

Klank hugs, squeezes, spins. He twists the Edison Antimatter Squirt Gun off its mount, redirecting its deadly beam in a dangerous arc that slices through the tops of the titanium bars, a stray tuft of hair on Watson's head, the middle of the boom with Edison still on it, and the very heart of the massive particle collider.

Dancing *whang, whang, whang* to his HEAVY METAL 2 beat, Klank hug-twirl falls, pulling the Edison Anti-matter Squirt Gun down on  top of himself. Klank gives one more max hug, and the cracking, smoking, sparking pistol erupts in a blinding white-light explosion, annihilating every bit of itself, the Antimatter Motor—and the robot Klank.

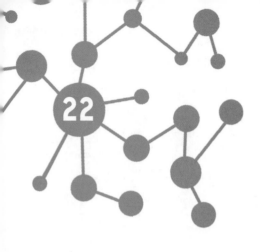

FRANK AND WATSON SIT AT THE LABORATORY WORKBENCH, FACING Frank's laptop screen.

"We are so sorry to hear you didn't win the Science Prize, sweetie."

Frank waves a hand. "Ah, don't worry about that, Mom. The science is more fun than any prize. And just this morning I sold a magnetic levitation idea to a cool skateboard company and paid off Grampa's deed, so we can keep the store."

"You sold a magnet?" says Mary Einstein. "For Grampa's steed?"

Frank laughs. "I'll explain it all when you get home."

Grampa Al pops his head in Frank's laboratory door. He calls, "Hi, Mary! Hi, Bob! Everything's copacetic. Now if you will excuse me, I've got bigger fish to fry."

"Huh?" says Watson. "What does that mean?"

"I'm making us dinner. Bye, Mary! Bye, son!" Grampa Al disappears into the kitchen.

Bob Einstein appears next to Mary. "We're back in the country, sport. So I'll be able to help you with your next invention!"

"Oh gosh, Dad. That is . . . uh . . . great."

Klink wheels up to the workbench. "Are you being sarcastic?"

"Wow," says Bob. "Did your Shop-Vac just say something?"

Klink beeps.

"Uh, more to explain when you guys get home. See you soon. Bye!"

Frank closes his laptop. He stacks his papers.

Watson wipes down a shelf. He organizes some tools.

Klink sits silently, his LED lights pulsing ever so slightly.

"Man, Edison sure was mad," says Watson.

"Mmm-hmm," agrees Frank, looking through his science encyclopedia.

"He is going to be your enemy for life."

"Uh-huh," agrees Frank, drawing a doodle.

"And that ape is not going to be your best friend either."

"Yeah."

It is suddenly very quiet in Frank Einstein's lab.

Watson picks up a copy of Klank's favorite Captain Underpants book. He frowns. "Einstein, sometimes I think *you* are a robot. Don't you miss Klank? He was a good guy."

Klink powers up. "A robot cannot be good or bad. Klank was a robot." Klink blinks once, then twice. "But I would like to try to understand his jokes again."

Frank looks up from his science book. "So our next subject is Energy. Here's what I'm thinking."

Watson stares at Frank. "Are you kidding? Klank blew himself up for us, and all you can think about is—"

There is a knock on the door leading out to the backyard.

"Oh, wait. Just a second." Frank gets up from the workbench.

A voice on the other side of the door says, **"Knock, knock."**

"Who's there?" asks Frank.

"Little old lady."

"Little old lady who?"

Frank swings open the door. Klank clomps in and booms: **"I did not know you could yodel!"**

"Klank!" yells Watson.

"Ha-ha-ha," beeps Klink.

Klank plods over to the workbench and wraps his aluminum flex arms around Watson, Klink, and a smiling Frank.

"Hugs! Give Klank hugs! Klank give hugs! Klank hugs give! Hugs Klank give!"

MATTER

ENERGY

HUMANS

Aristotle

$E=mc^2$

Before anyone can ask any questions, Frank answers, "*Re-assembled* artificial intelligence. With just a little help from me. Though we still couldn't find much memory or brain power."

Klank holds up his new pipe-wrench hand. **"But we did find this! Klank is now bigger and better than ever!"**

Everyone laughs. Even Klink. Kind of.

LIFE

EARTH

UNIVERSE

Frank looks over this strange group. He says:

"**RESULTS:** Three good friends. Grampa Al's place is safe . . . for now. May have a lifelong enemy in T. Edison."

Frank looks up at the Wall of Science.

"**CONCLUSION:** Matter and antimatter—amazing."

Frank pauses for a second.

"Now, about that *energy* idea. I have an invention that just might be even more amazing. Who's with me?"

Watson smiles. "Count me in."

"Me too," beeps Klink.

"Me three!" boom-chicka-boom-booms Klank.

"All in," says Frank Einstein.

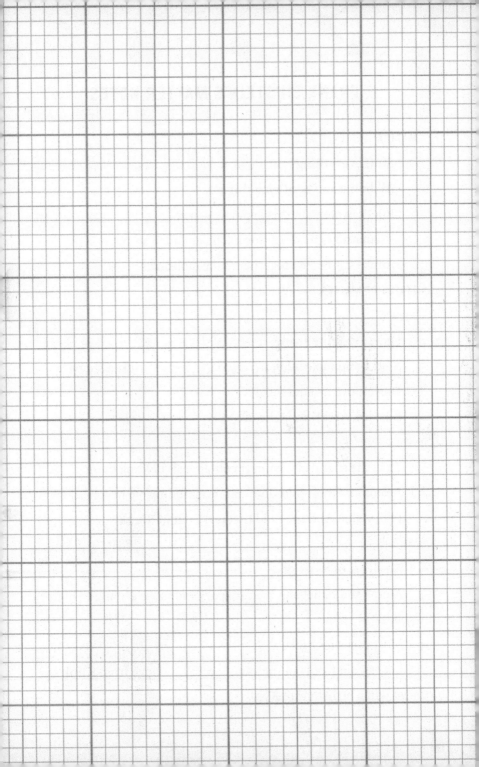

FRANK EINSTEIN'S MATTER NOTES

MATTER

Stuff everything is made of.

All living and nonliving things.

Rocks, water, air, this paper, you, me.

All matter is made of tiny particles called atoms.

Atoms connected together make molecules.

STATES OF MATTER

SOLIDS

Have a definite shape.

Atoms and molecules arranged in a tightly packed shape.

Don't move around much.

Like ice. And Klank's head.

LIQUIDS

Take the shape of whatever container is holding them.

Atoms and molecules move around, sliding over each other.

Like water. And the fluid that leaks out of Klank.

GAS

No shape of its own.

Atoms and molecules are far apart and move around at high speed.

Most gases invisible.

Like steam from boiling water. And the smoke from Klink's head when he listens to Klank.

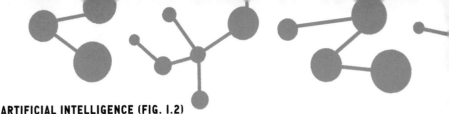

ARTIFICIAL INTELLIGENCE (FIG. I.2)

A machine that can do the things humans do.

See *Klink*.

ARTIFICIAL *ALMOST* INTELLIGENCE (FIG. I.3)

A machine that can do some of the things humans do, only not very well.

But usually pretty good at joke telling and making music.

See *Klank*.

COW METHANE (FIG. I.7)

Gas. Produced by cows' digestion.

A molecule made of 1 carbon atom and 4 hydrogen atoms.

Released into the air mostly by cow burps. But also by cow farts.

Estimated 250 liters per cow per day.

That's 250 liter-sized bottles. Full. Of. Cow. Gas.

ATOM (FIGS. I.II AND I.12)

Particle that makes up all matter.

So small it would take millions of atoms to make a dot on this page.

Main particles of the atom are protons, neutrons, and electrons.

Some matter— gold, copper, and silver—has just one kind of atom.

Other matter—water—is made of different atoms that are connected.

Connected atoms are called molecules.

ANTIMATTER (FIG. 1.13)

Universe made of matter, but scientists have done experiments that show antimatter exists too.

Antimatter has opposite electrical charge of matter.

When matter meets its antimatter, they destroy each other . . . and release a lot of energy.

Should be just as much antimatter as matter in the universe, since both were created equally when the universe began in the Big Bang (say, 13.82 billion years ago).

No one has been able to find much antimatter.

Scientists at CERN and other places are producing antimatter by smashing atomic particles together.

MOLECULE (FIG. 1.16)

Different atoms connected to make a substance.

Water is molecules of 2 hydrogen atoms with 1 oxygen atom. Written as H_2O.

Methane gas is 1 atom of carbon with 4 hydrogen atoms. Written as CH_4.

CERN (FIG. 1.21)

Research center near Geneva, Switzerland. Scientists from a bunch of countries built a machine that speeds up atomic particles in a giant underground ring . . . and then smashes them into each other.

Scientists trying to learn more about how atoms, and the universe, are made.

Biggest man-made machine ever, built to study smallest particles of matter.

Named the Large Hadron Collider.

Underground ring is so big it crosses the border of France and Switzerland four times.

A WATSON FAVORITE INVENTION

I.00: CHANGING STATES OF MATTER: THE POPSICLE

When Frank Epperson was eleven years old in San Francisco in 1905, he left a stirring stick in a pot of flavored soda water on an outdoor porch.

That night, the temperature went down below freezing (32 degrees Fahrenheit, 0 degrees Celsius). The water changed states from liquid to solid ice.

The next morning, Frank picked up the stick, and the whole block of flavored ice came with it.

Eighteen years later Frank remembered his frozen treat on a stick. He registered his idea with the patent office and called his invention the Epsicle.

But Frank's kids called him Pop. And they called his invention by a better name—the Popsicle.

KLINK AND KLANK PRESENT
HOW TO MAKE YOUR OWN ANTIMATTER MOTOR

INGREDIENTS

    1 dropper of water (H_2O)

    1 dropper of antiwater (anti-H_2O)

EQUIPMENT

    1 old bicycle, 1 lawn mower motor, 2 extension cords, 3 copper
tubes, magnets, detectors, shielding, storage rings

I. ASSEMBLE INGREDIENTS AND EQUIPMENT IN YOUR LABORATORY.

2. MAKE ANTIWATER BY FIRST—

"Hey, Klink!"

"Klank, why are you interrupting? We are ex-
plaining how to make an Antimatter Motor."

**"I know, I know. But this is just like matter
and antimatter."**

"Is it really?"

"Yes, really."

"It is not another knock-knock
joke?"

"No, it is not."

"Are you positive?"

"Yes."

"It better not be."

"Robot's honor. This is not a knock-knock joke."

"OK. What is it?"

"So there are these two robots named Pete and Re-Pete. They are sitting on a wall. Pete falls off. Who is left?"

"Re-Pete."

"So there are these two robots named Pete and Re-Pete. They are sitting on a wall. Pete falls off. Who is left?"

"Re-Pete."

"So there are these two ro-bots named Pete and Re-Pete. They are sitting on a wall. Pete falls off. Who is left?"

"Re-Pete."

"So there are these two robots named Pete and Re-Pete. They are sitting on a wall. Pete falls off. Who is left?"

"Re-Pete."

"So there are these two robots named Pete and Re-

T. EDISON'S NEW INVENTIONS

5D TV:

AIR TEXT:

LASER MOVIE PROJECTOR:

NO-BULB LIGHT:

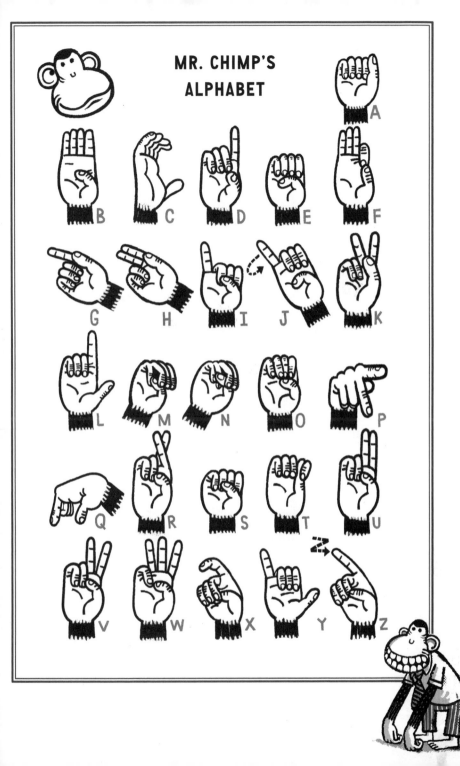

MR. CHIMP'S ALPHABET

JON SCIESZKA grew up loving science. Some of his early groundbreaking science fair work, placing celery stalks in colored water, is still referenced today (by his mom). He is the author of *The True Story of the 3 Little Pigs!*, *The Stinky Cheese Man and Other Fairly Stupid Tales*, *Battle Bunny*, the Time Warp Trio series, and too many other books to list. He is also the founder of Guys Read. Scieszka served as the first National Ambassador for Young People's Literature. He lives in Brooklyn, New York, and still loves science.

BRIAN BIGGS has illustrated books by Garth Nix, Cynthia Rylant, and Katherine Applegate, and is the writer and illustrator of the Everything Goes series. He lives in Philadelphia.